On
The Other
Side Of
Space

NELLOTIE CHASTAIN

WESTBOW
PRESS®
A DIVISION OF THOMAS NELSON
& ZONDERVAN

WestBow Press books may be ordered through booksellers or by contacting:

WestBow Press
A Division of Thomas Nelson & Zondervan
1663 Liberty Drive
Bloomington, IN 47403
www.westbowpress.com
844-714-3454

ISBN: 979-8-3850-2868-9 (sc)
ISBN: 979-8-3850-2869-6 (e)

Library of Congress Control Number: 2024913170

Print information available on the last page.

WestBow Press rev. date: 07/23/2024

Dedication

On The Other Side Of Space is dedicated to Mary Breckinridge.
I did not have the privilege of meeting Mary Breckinridge,
but, along with my parents, visited her place in Kentucky many
times. My stepmother, Virginia Larson Porter, worked for the
Frontier Nursing Service for many years. Always impressed
by and thankful for the services Mary Breckinridge began and
carried through to her death, I am equally grateful for how
she set up the services to be carried on through forever.

Born in Memphis, Tennessee on February 17, 1881, Mary
Breckinridge grew up in Washington, D.C. where her father served as
U.S. minister to Russia. She attended school in Lausanne, Switzerland,
and Stamford, Connecticut. After her husband's death in 1906, she
attended St. Luke's Hospital School of Nursing, graduating in 1910 as
an R.N..

Devastated by the deaths of her newborn daughter and her for-year-
old son, she made the decision to honor their memory by devoting her
life to improving children's conditions

Beginning her work in 1928 in Hyden, Leslie County, Kentucky,
she founded the Frontier Nursing Service which, for several years,
was entirely underwritten by her personal funds. Designed around
the central hospital with only one physician and nursing outposts to
compensate for the absence of reliable roads or transportation. For

many years, the service featured nurses on horseback that could reach the most remote areas.

The hospital in Hyden is now named the Mary Breckinridge Hospital and has a Women's Health Care Center that fulfills Mary Breckinridge's mission created in the 1920s.

The introduction of nurse-midwives into the region brough its maternal and neonatal death rates well below the national average. In addition to directing the service, which led to the foundation in 1929 of the American Association of Nurse-Midwives, she also edited its journal and traveled around the country as a fund-raiser. Breckinridge's autobiography, *Wide Neighborhoods: A Story of the Frontier Nursing Service*, was published in 1952.

On her deathbed Mary Breckinridge commented, "The glorious thing about it is that it has worked."

CHAPTER 1

"Maybe I'll stop in for a visit." Like a kiss on ice skates, her tear dampened giggle whispered across black granite. On each side of the stone was a rose bush full of tiny buds edged in deep black red.

STEPHEN NOLAN
October 10, 2000 –October 10, 2027
Father of Nathan

NATHAN NOLAN
January 9, 2024 - October 10, 2027
Son of Steven and Nicole

Heaven Is Blessed

Jim knew where to find his daughter. "I'll have her home on time. Not to worry."

Monica's damp lashes lay on her cheeks as his lips soothed her creased forehead.

"Thanks, honey. Don't forget your flashlight, just in case," she said.

Using her apron to dry her cheeks, she watched her husband back out of the driveway. "It's been two years, God, when does the healing happen?"

"Soon."

"Excuse me?" She spun to an empty kitchen. Her hand rested over her heart as she sank into a chair. "Oh." Her awe filled whisper floated toward the spackled ceiling.

Jim, retired from a lifetime of building and repairing homes, and

Monica Amburgy, who had chosen the life of a housewife and mother, were now living in their daughter's home.

After Nicol's first interview in Houston, she had roared back into life like a rampant forest fire, burning her path toward space. Not ready to give up the home she shared with Stephen and Nathan, Nicol convinced her parents to put their house on the market and move into hers.

Basking in the security of her parents' love on each of her visits home during her training, assured her their decision had been the right one. She was now ready to step into the next phase of her training.

Jim and Monica were waiting to drive their daughter to the Lexington, Kentucky airport after a late dinner. Her bags waited on the porch, but where was Nicol?

Just like many times before, he found the Jeep parked behind their small, white church that hugged the mountain where a cedar-chip path led to the cemetery. Each time he found her like this, pain stabbed his heart like the thrust of a saber.

Nicol sat cross-legged on the dew-damp sod. Her fingers remained buried in the soft earth as she fought the urge to dig through to the custom built casket that cushioned her husband in whose arm her son would eternally sleep.

"Nici." Jim's voice matched his soft grip on her shoulders. "Mom has supper ready."

"Daddy, I'm sorry." As if already moving in the vacuum of space, her body rolled into her father's arms.

Settling on knee on the soft grass, Jim kept his arm around her. Knowing his one and only child would be at the Galaxy Space Center before daylight, he chewed on his lower lip.

"You still sure this is what you want to do, honey?" he asked.

"Yes. It's just difficult leaving them, you know, Daddy."

"I know, sweetie." He caressed her hair.

"You'll take care of them for me, won't you?" she whispered.

"Just like always."

"I just told them that I might stop in for a visit." Her giggle pulled a smile across his face.

"Well, darlin', if you do, tell them I said "howdy.""

She suddenly hopped to her feet and reached for his hand. "Come on, let's go eat. I've got a plane waiting for me."

"My daughter the astronaut; who would have thought?"

Arm in arm, they walked toward their vehicles. Snatched by angels, their laughter was carried across earth's boundaries.

CHAPTER 2

Nicol's childhood dreams had never included soaring through space, or donning a Pillsbury doughboy suit and walking through the darkness of space, or becoming a hostess in the shuttle that transported vacationers on their voyage through the stars.

Born in the Mary Breckinridge Hospital in Hyden, Kentucky, Nicol Amburgy was a natural beauty that drew attention, even as an infant. Her smile was like an explosion of sunshine.

Looking into her eyes was like looking into the deepest part of the sea. Her thick, dark hair bounced along the shoulder blades of her five foot five stature.

In October of her senior year at Leslie County High School, Nicol was crowned Queen of the annual Mary Breckinridge Festival.

The small town of Hyden, Kentucky, the birthplace of midwifery and family nursing in America, celebrates the life of Mary Breckinridge and her contributions to the area with an annual festival.

Born in 1881, Mary Breckinridge's life changed forever after the death of her first husband and her two children from her second marriage. She found the comfort and strength she needed to survive in nursing. After years of study and training, Mary Breckinridge became the founder of The Frontier Nursing Service in Leslie County, Kentucky, the largest midwifery educational facility in the United States today.

Although Nicol excelled in each of her first twelve years of school, her number one dream was to be a wife and a mother. She graduated from high school at sixteen and two years later had earned a Bachelor of Science degree.

Just as the catalyst of pain motivated Mary Breckinridge into her field of service, Nicol Amburgy Nolan's splintered spirit catapulted her into the new and improved space program.

CHAPTER 3

The events on October 10, 2027, ripped the smile from Nicol's face and left the haunt of death in her eyes. Too far away to hear when a monstrous coal truck slammed head-on into the GMC Jimmy driven by Stephen Nolan with three year old Nathan buckled safely into his padded booster seat behind Stephen, her heart felt it.

"Sweetie, your son wants to buy his mommy some strawberry ice cream for my birthday. Be back in a jiff." Stephen's voice slid under the closed bathroom door and dripped into the tub of bubbles she soaked in.

"Come give me sugar first."

"Ice cream, Mommy." Nathan's hands scooped bubbles when Stephen lifted him for mommy's kiss.

"Thank you, darlin'," she said. "I can't wait."

"Me either." Stephen's eyes let her know it wasn't about ice cream.

"'mon, Daddy."

"Save some bubbles." His kiss had been deep and hot.

"Sure. You can clean the tub." Her wet arms wrapped around his neck. "I love you."

"M-m-m. And I love you."

Full of life; full of love; full of anticipation, her two men hurried out of the steamy room.

Later, with a red, white, and blue afghan wrapped around her pink nightgown, she waited on the couch; sated with happiness, her eyelids drooped.

At the moment of impact seven miles away, her eyes popped open. In the fog of drowsiness, she jumped up, tossing the afghan. She felt her heart knock against her ribs.

"7:05. They should be back." Her voice trembled.

Jerking open the door, she rushed onto the porch. The yard, the driveway, Highway 421 were all far too dark.

Near the mouth of Camp Creek, Stephen and Nicol's brick-faced home sat 200 feet back from Highway 421–far enough for Nathan to be safe when he was outside playing.

As if she had just finished a marathon, her heart continued to pound. Long, agonizing minutes passed before headlights turned onto the driveway. She smiled in relief until the porch light reflected off the light bar of the police car.

Like fingernails across a blackboard, her screams ripped through the night.

Pulling into the driveway directly behind the sheriff, Nicol's parents ran to their daughter before the sheriff reached the porch.

Stephen was one of the sheriff's deputies. His chest ached as if an elephant were sitting on him, knowing that no amount of gentleness could cushion the message that Nicol's reasons for living were on their way to the county morgue.

A top executive in the mining company that owned most of the local coal mines, Stephen's father had re-located his family to Leslie County when Stephen was beginning his junior year in high school.

Six foot tall and dark headed, Stephen Nolan was not considered particularly handsome to most of the female students in Leslie County High School. But within his first weeks at the school, Nicol Amburgy had been captured by the mystery in his dark eyes. By the end of the first semester of his senior year, they were engaged.

Both determined to gain the benefits of college before they married. Stephen pursued his dream of being in law enforcement. Other than her dream of becoming a wife and mother, Nicol couldn't quite decide what her college major should be, but after two years of hard work, she had an Associate Degree in Science.

After the accident, Nicol moved through life as a zombie, trapped in a nightmare from which there was no escape. Stephen, her husband of three short years and her reason to live, was gone. Nathan, her three year old son and her reason to breathe, was gone. On days when the sun shone brightest, she only saw darkness.

Standing at the kitchen sink washing one cereal bowl, one spoon, and one glass, she glanced out the window. Suddenly, her black and white world switched to color. Dogwood and Red Bud trees painted the mountain behind her house white, pink, and brilliant red.

Running out the door onto the porch, her voice trembled as her arm folded around the porch post. "Stephen, can you see it?"

Only when it had been necessary during those twelve dark months, Nicol visited the grocery store. Snatching her purse, she ran to her Jeep and headed into town, her eyes dancing from the road up the sides of the mountain and down to the river.

The Jeep drank a tank full of fuel as Nicol listened to the songs of birds as if she'd never heard them before. As she paid for the fuel, she grabbed three newspapers, a candy bar, and a soda pop.

Returning home, she scooted into the porch swing that had only been used in the middle of those nights when she had been unable to sleep. The swing squawked as she hungrily perused each of the newspapers.

Four rose bushes in front of the porch were bursting with buds and early blossoms. Miniature rose bushes had been Mother's Day gifts from Stephen. With each bush, he had placed a tiny rose petal in her hand. "Just one petal; a tiny drop of my love." The aroma from her favorite deep crimson flowers wafted across the swing. Nicol smiled.

Three pages into the national news section, her eyes were drawn like magnets to an ad that she read three times. The space program, being revamped by private entities, was looking for qualified volunteers to train for host and hostess positions aboard the space shuttle which would now transport vacationers into space.

Nicol remembered sitting in Louisville's IMAX theater watching

"Hubble" and being proud that the astronomer the Hubble telescope was named for and the astronaut whose space walk helped fix the telescope's initial problems had ties to Kentucky.

Years earlier the United States space shuttle program was basically closed down. But when the idea arose to shuttle civilians into space, the program was revived and moved forward quickly.

There had been no reason for Nicol to give any thought to the space program—until now. Like a paper magnet, the ad kept dragging her eyes back to it.

One month passed and then another, but that section of the paper still lay on the table, ragged from being folded and refolded every day.

"Look! I'm going to do it," she said aloud after breakfast three months later.

With a blank legal pad and a pen, Nicol sat at the table with her cell phone. When the call ended, the top page was filled with notes. At the bottom of the page, an appointment for her first interview for the position of astronaut hostess was circled in red. Nicol Amburgy Nolan had taken her first giant step into space.

CHAPTER 4

What began as twelve months of training passed as quickly as a light-year. She dove into training like a pelican into a school of fish. Her mind, body, and spirit were open to everything from book work to the physical requirements that would lead to her first flight into space.

Although the training for shuttle host and hostess positions wasn't the same caliber as former astronauts had, Nicol was determined to be prepared for anything and everything that might become necessary while gliding through the adventures of space.

Like a gung-ho soldier during basic training, Nicol sailed through boot camp where she learned about the refurbished shuttle, new space station systems, and all the other necessary disciplines such as Earth sciences, meteorology, space science and engineering.

Nicol Nolan's exuberance in training and the manner in which she mastered each step in the schedule drew notice and she was the first trainee to be given clearance for short walks in space. The first civilian vacation shuttle adventure was scheduled for 2037.

Plans were in place for civilian space vacationers who had paid the exorbitant additional fee to be taken outside by an astronaut, were excited to have Nicol, the only hostess trained for space walks.

Although those days were long past, Nicol wished she could still take part in the research with the CubeLab modules that had been placed on the space station years earlier by a joint mission with NanoRacks and Kentucky Space.

Nicol was on her way to The Galaxy Training center, the renamed Sonny Carter Training Facility, where deep in the 6.2 million gallon pool, that was more than 200 feet long and 40 feet deep, she would train for space walks.

Galaxy Adventures, the consortium that now owned and operated what used to be the United States Space Program, provided delivery service to the expanded international space station that now had a wing specifically used for short-term vacationers.

Most of the same training, including physiological and psychological support the original astronauts went through, was still required for the shuttle crews because, even with the amazing changes that had developed over the years, space was still a hazardous environment that the crews needed to be prepared for.

Since her first day of training, anxiety was nonexistent for Nicol. That is, until her first immersion into what the trainees called the Swimming Hole. Her breaths threatened to fog her face shield. Her heart rate accelerated as if she were jogging, pumping her blood pressure up the scale. The monitors were watched closely, ready to extract her from her forty feet deep classroom.

Like the quiet in deep ocean depths, Nicol calmed, pulling in a deep breath. Thumbs pointed to the monitor room ceiling.

George Surface stayed close to his student as she began the last leg of her training before soaring into space. His confidence level in her was high. Never before had any trainee aced every aspect of the training program like she had. Her mesmerizing beauty only added to her mystic.

Her vivacious personality drew almost everyone she met into her friendship pool. Most of the seven other hostess trainees were grateful for Nicol's encouragements along the way. Realizing early in the training that they would never surpass her, the four male trainees settled for friendly competition with her.

Driven by her determination to meet her own goals, Nicol spent much less time in leisure entertainment than the other trainees. Her visits back home were few. The emptiness in the center of her heart remained deep and black as space.

Nicol's surge toward her goal left her little emotional space for best friends. Sandra, the youngest of the trainees, idolized Nicol, determined to be the watcher of her back. Cybil, exceptionally beautiful with long red hair and emerald, green eyes, was within an inch of being too tall for the mission. Outwardly praising Nicol for her accomplishments, inside jealousy writhed like a nest of asps.

Dalyn's skin was black as Kentucky coal. Rarely finding faults in anyone, her perky personality drew friends like bees to an apple blossom. Jaylee, quiet and highly intelligent, was best buddies with Dalyn.

Sandra and Barbara looked forward to the bi-monthly pizza bashes as the girls celebrate the conquest of each week's obstacles.

Nearing the end of her first two months at the Galaxy Training Center, Nicol stopped long enough to call Dalyn on her cell phone and make plans for their pizza party.

"Hey, Dalyn, how's it going?" Nicol asked.

"Nicol, I didn't expect to hear from you so soon. What's up?"

"I've come up for air and I'm needing pizza badly. We still on?" Nicol asked.

"Yes, ma'am. I'll let the rest of the gang know. Same place?"

"That'd be great. See you there." Nicol smiled as she punched in her parents' number.

"How do you do that?" Barbara asked. Her short, bleach-blond hair was spiked on top, exposing the tip of a purple-black tail that slithered down the back of her neck to the head of a smiling dragon. The happy ophidian tattoo remained hidden during training by the high collar of her jumpsuit. Black eyeliner ringed her hazel eyes.

"What?" Nicol mumbled through a mouth full of pizza.

"How do you put away so much pizza and not pop out the seams on your suit?"

"Are you kidding," Cybil said. "You know how many hours she spends in workout." Her smiling lips, coated with bronze gloss, belied the daggers shooting from her green eyes in Nicol's direction.

Sandra's face fired to red. Seeing the depth of contempt in Cybil's eyes, she intended to relay a warning to Nicol but the pizza stopped her. Grabbing Cybil's forearm, her fingernails sank like fish hooks.

"Ouch!" Cybil yelped. Grabbing Sandra's hand, she squeezed.

"No, she's choking," Dalyn yelled.

Cybil loosed her hold on Sandra's hand when Dalyn rushed behind Sandra and grabbed her around the abdomen. One jerk removed the obstruction. Tears ran from Sandra's eyes as she gasped life back into her lungs.

"Thank you," she rasped.

"Sandra, are you all right?" Nicol folded her young friend into her arms.

"Gross," Cybil mumbled, rubbing the blood from her forearm.

After a swift cleanup of the expelled chunk of pizza, Jaylee shoved clean napkins to Nicol.

Gently wiping Sandra's face, Nicol smiled. "That's not how I do it."

As if Sandra's giggle gave permission, Dalyn and Barbara's laughter mushroomed into a cloud of happiness.

Cybil snatched her shoulder bag from the back of her chair and abruptly left the break room.

Feeling as if her dragon had come to life and was writhing down her back, Barbara's eyes closed.

Laughter slowly subsided, followed by short bursts of giggles as the girls plopped into their original chairs. Nicol picked up slice number four and cleared her throat before biting off the pointed edge. Like Christmas silver bells, giggles tinkled through every corner of the room.

Swigging her diet cola, Sandra's eyes caught the fear in Barbara's as she sat with her back straight against her chair. She knows.

As nonchalantly as possible, she leaned close enough to whisper. "You saw?"

Fresh tears tumbled onto Barbara's napkin as she nodded. Emptying her water bottle, she mouthed, "Talk later?"

One nod was all the answer she needed.

"Well ladies, this has been great. I think I will run a few laps then hit the sack. Good night," Nicol said.

"Nite."

"Goodnight."

At the door, Nicol stopped and turned. "You all are great friends." She disappeared down the hallway.

Lagging behind, Sandra and Barbara finished tidying up the break room before sitting across the table from each other.

"I have to hit the little girls room," Jaylee announced before disappearing out the door.

"What do we do, Sandra," Barbara asked. "Cybil's hate was hot as a rocket's blast."

"I've seen it before, Barb, even though she's been good at hiding it," Sandra said.

"Should we talk to someone, just in case?" Barbara's fingers rubbed the back of her neck.

"That's just it," Sandra said. "As far as I know, it's just looks. What can they do about that?"

"But what if she sabotages Nicol's equipment or something?" Barbara said.

Sandra rubbed her temples. "Okay, let's keep our eyes open and try not to let Nicol out of our sight. If we see anything, anything at all, we'll talk to George."

"Sounds good." Barbara leaned forward to whisper. "I think George likes Nicol anyway."

"You picked up on that, too?" Sandra's mouth pulled into a sideways smile.

"You think maybe?" Barbara asked, her eye brows arched.

"I don't know," Sandra said. "Nicol hasn't been interested in men since losing her husband."

"But that was so long ago," Barbara said. "Maybe it's about time."

"George does seem to be a nice man," Sandra said. "He's definitely the most gorgeous man in this facility, even if he is an officer."

Pushing forty, Commander George Surface could easily be mistaken for a movie star. Salt and pepper hair topped a five ten, one hundred eighty pound tightly packed body. "Eye candy" was whispered between the female trainees as they traversed the hallways. The ladies knew he was unmarried, but never saw him with a woman.

"Remember the pinky pact we used to make as kids?" Sandra asked.

"How can I forget?" Barbara smiled.

"Let's make a pinky pack to pray for Nicol's protection from any harm, especially from a jealous red head."

Their pinkies hooked as their hands pumped up and down.

As quietly as a moth, Jaylee floated down the long, gray hallway. Slipping into the ladies room, she checked each of the twelve stalls. Pulling the last door back into place, she noticed it to be heavier.

"That's odd," she whispered. Stepping into the stall, she shut the door to discover Cybil's bag hanging on the purse hook. Pursing her lips, she lifted the bag from the hook but changed her mind. Slowly, she slipped the purse handle back over the hook.

This bag isn't important. Where Cybil is, that's important.

Easing through silence, she pulled the restroom door open. The hall was empty. As she walked toward the light shining through the gym doors at the end of the hallway, she checked each strategically placed security camera.

Pushing through the doors, she smiled and waved. On her last lap, Nicol waved back. George Surface, the four male trainees, two of the secretaries, and Cybil were involved in a heated basketball game.

Nicol finished her lap, wiped her face with a towel, and began stretching her legs. Jaylee saw Commander Surface miss the basketball when he turned to watch Nicol.

"Thought you could use this about now," Jaylee said, handing a water bottle to Nicol.

"Bless your heart," Nicol said. "This is exactly what I need." She twisted off the lid, failing to notice how easily it twisted, and lifted the bottle toward her lips. In a splattered second, the bottle sailed across the floor.

"Ouch!" Nicol yelped, grabbing her elbow.

"Hey, you idiot," Jaylee shouted.

"I'm sorry. Are you all right?" George Surface held Nicol's arm while everyone rushed over.

"Oh, sir, I am so sorry," Jaylee began before being cut off.

"Not a problem," George said, not bothering to look in Jaylee's direction. "Nicol, I am sorry. It was an accident."

"I realize that, sir," she said. "It startled me more than anything."

"Actually, it was a diversion to keep us from beating them," Cybil yelled from middle court.

One of the men dribbled the ball across the floor as the game continued. George stayed next to Nicol.

"Really, sir, I'm fine," Nicol said. "Just a little thirsty." Her laugh was light and sweet.

George smiled as he reached into a small cooler and pulled out a frosty bottle, twisted off the cap and handed it to her.

Taking a long drink, Nicol signed. "Oh my, that's good."

"Sure you're okay?" Jaylee asked.

"Yes, Jaylee, I am," Nicol answered. "Thank you for thinking about me and I'm sorry it got wasted." She nodded toward the first bottle.

"Hey, that doesn't matter as long as you're all right," Jaylee said.

"Yes, ma'am, I'm fine," Nicol gave her a quick hug. "Sorry, I probably don't smell too good right now."

"I'll be going then," Jaylee said. "Unless you want me to wait and walk back with you."

"No, I'll be fine," Nicol said. "Thanks, though."

Jaylee quickly exited the gym but leaned against the wall; her teeth ground together. After a cloak and dagger look inside the gym, she stomped down the hallway.

George was still beside Nicol. Cybil was playing basketball but keeping her eye on Nicol.

"We'll see," Jaylee muttered. "We'll see."

Like a deflating balloon, Nicol soon felt the need to call it a night. Even though Cybil preferred to remain in the gym, just in case George returned, Nathan Herald, one of the crew, and George insisted on walking Nicol and Cybil to their vehicles.

Just before entering her car, Cybil pulled her ponytail loose and shook her hair around her shoulders before turning to smile at George. His eyes were on Nicol's Mustang as it pulled away. Cybil's vehicle door slammed.

CHAPTER 5

Her final visit to the cemetery before her maiden walk in space was bitter sweet as she shared her plans with Stephen and Nathan.

"Steve, I need to ask you something, just in case." Her hands rubbed the sides of her denim covered legs. "If, and it's a big if, but if someone were to become interested in me, you know, as a woman, date, wife, would I have your blessing? I've not given much thought to this kind of thing, but there is someone who I think might be interested. He seems like a fine man. I just don't know. I'm afraid, actually.

I miss you so much and I'll love you forever, but the loneliness clouds my life sometimes. If this should ever happen, could you somehow let me know if it's okay or not? Could you somehow give me your blessing?" Her hand caressed the black stone.

She sat crossed-legged in front of the stone and ran her finger over her son's name. "I wonder what it's like on the other side of space," she whispered.

"Nathan, you're not going to believe what your Mommy's getting ready to do." Her diaphragm contracted as her breath stopped: her battle not to cry was close to being lost. Her eyes lifted to the cotton-ball clouds. One lone tear tumbled down the side of her face.

"Remember? I told you I might stop in for a visit." She smiled as she whispered, "I'll be close enough and, oh, how I wished I could."

Tipping on to her knees, her lips kissed the cool granite of "Stephen" before lingering almost too long on "Nathan."

Standing at the foot of the grave site with her hands rammed into her pockets, she whispered, "I'll love you forever."

She turned to leave the cemetery. One by one, the petals withered and dropped from the rose bush on Stephen's side of the stone. A swish of cold air brushed her face as she slid into her vehicle.

Monica, unable to join Jim and their daughter on their way to the airport, dampened her husband's handkerchief with her tears. Pride in Nicol's accomplishments was shrouded in the darkness of her fear-filled test of faith.

Deep shadows crossed the yard and crept over the porch as the time passed like a sluggish drain. "I can't lose her, too, God. Please, keep her safe."

Dusk peppered the mountain. Monica's chest felt as if a massive rubber band was squeezing away her breath when the front room shone with the brilliance of the Nativity Star. Her hand gripped the front of her Kentucky sweatshirt.

"She's mine to touch; she's mine to heal. Trust me?" The depth of compassion in the words, snapped the band of fear. With no thought to her badly sprained ankle, she slid from the couch to her knees.

With her forehead touching the couch cushion, her tears of fear turned to warm tears of holy gratitude. "Yes," she whispered. "Jesus, thank you."

Minutes passed; in the sacred second before darkness filled the room like soft black cotton, she felt a feathered touch on her ankle. Pulling herself back onto the couch, she sat in the softness of peace until she slipped into the healing depth of sleep.

"Daddy, I'm going to be fine. My excitement far surpasses any fear. Please don't worry about me. God is still my pilot."

"I know, darlin'. I have to say, though, that you've never been this far away from us before." A sob escaped his tight throat as his arms around her tightened like an octopus' tentacle.

"Daddy, I'll see you real soon, I promise." Using her wadded up tissue, she wiped his eyes.

Nodding, he smiled. "I know, darlin'. Don't pay any attention to a blubbering, old man."

"Yeah, there's no way on God's green earth that you could be labeled as "old." Her giggle made him laugh.

Everyone had already boarded; the attendants gently advised them the plane would be leaving in minutes.

"Gotta, go, Daddy. See you soon."

"Darlin' remember that I'll love you always," he called as she reached the curve of the loading platform that would take her inside the plane.

Wiping his face with his handkerchief, he turned to leave. "I'll love you for eternity, my darlin' girl."

CHAPTER 6

Parked under the security light, Nicole's Mustang GT convertible shone like onyx.

"Midnight," she moaned as she handed the fare, plus tip, over the front seat. The cabby thanked her and hurried out his door to retrieve her bags from the trunk. The ride from the airport to her apartment had been too short for a nap.

Sliding out of the cab, she stretched the tightness from her shoulders. Suddenly, she cried, "No!"

"What?" With a suitcase in each hand the cabbie spun around.

Ragged edges of the shredded convertible top flapped in the breeze.

"No, not my baby." Tears ran down Nicol's cheeks as she reached out to touch her car as if it were a beloved pet.

"No, don't touch it. Let me call the police," the cabbie said while he punched in three numbers and waited.

"This is your car?" he asked. His whistle brought the slightest of smiles to Nicol's distressed face.

"Why?" she moaned. "Why would anyone do something so cruel?"

"I thought security was tight around this place," he said.

Nicol looked at him. "You're right. So, how could this happen right here under their noses?"

"That'd be a good question for them when they do show up," he barked.

Security vehicles skidded to a halt in front of the taxi and beside the Mustang. Spotlights illuminated the area, exaggerating the gaping hole in her car.

After the initial round of facts was given to the officers, Nicol asked, "Can you tell me how this could happen with all the security that supposed to be around here?"

As if ignoring her question, the officer asked, "Do you have any enemies?"

"Enemies?" she asked. "Are you serious? Officer, I've never had an enemy in my entire life."

"That you know of," he remarked as he made a lap around the Mustang.

Her perfectly arched eyebrows pulled together.

"Listen, Miss..." his eyes dropped to his clipboard. "Nolan. Considering who you are, what you do, and where this occurred tells me this is more than mere vandalism."

The second officer finished taking pictures and began dusting gray dust onto the jet-black vehicle.

"But who?" Nicol wondered out loud.

"That's what we'll try our best to find out. So, you're going up there?" His thumb pointed upward.

"Yes, sir."

"Impressive." Respect infused his voice. "When?"

"Two weeks from Monday."

"Good luck," he said with a smile.

"Thanks, but I prefer faith to luck?"

"One more reason to find the answers we need," he said. "I'll need a list of everyone in this apartment building."

"But, Officer..."

"Embree. Duane Embree, ma'am."

"Officer Embree, they are all my friends and co-workers," she said. "In fact, some of them will be going up with me."

His eyebrows and shoulders rose.

"Okay," she whispered. Tears quickly filled her eyes. "You'll have the list tomorrow." Her mind raced through the names and faces she knew to be in the building—her friends.

"Here's my card," he said, placing the card in her trembling fingers. "Call me when you have the list."

"Thank you, sir." Her handshake was surprisingly firm.

"You can call me Duane. And I'm sorry this has happened to one of our finest."

"Thank you." Her damp eyes smiled.

In the nano second before he turned, his eyes caught the flutter of a curtain in a third floor window. He mentally filed the information.

"I'll wait here for the tow truck if you want to take your bags inside."

Tucking his six foot, two hundred pound frame into his vehicle after Nicol entered the building, Officer Embree jotted down the number of the window on the third floor.

Nicol walked out of the building just as the tow truck arrived. Tears dampened her cheeks as she watched her beloved Mustang being hauled away.

With one last look at the third floor window, he muttered, "Hurt her and you'll pay."

CHAPTER 7

After the final fitting for the space suits, Commander Surface brought in the astronauts and the female hostesses for a briefing on the new and improved suits that would be used solely for the space walks.

Design advancements in the EVA suits not only fulfilled the requirements to keep an astronaut alive and comfortable in the severe environment of outer space, they were now designed with an extra safety element that would supply life support to the space walkers for an added two hours if connection to the shuttle were to be lost.

"Other than in our training laboratories, this particular safety element would not be tested in outer space unless the ultimate accident should happen. Are there any questions?"

Nicol's heart rate accelerated. "How likely will it be for an accident such as this to happen?"

"We've never experienced one, nor do we expect to. This is just a new safety feature that has been built into our new suits that, in our best judgment, will never be put to use."

"Thank you, sir," she said. "I think I speak for everyone in this room when I say that we will hold you to that judgment."

Nervous laughter jogged across the room.

"These days will be busy, so follow the guidelines for getting your personal issues in order."

As the men exited the room, Commander Surface stopped Nicol.

"Nicol, I would like a word with you in my office before you leave the building."

"Certainly, sir. Now?"

"Fifteen minutes?"

"Thank you, sir. Fifteen minutes will be perfect." She rushed down the hall to the ladies room.

Stephen, I need you. Staring at herself in the mirror, she sucked in a deep breath, held it, then let it escape slowly. Raking her fingers through her shoulder-length hair, she leaned close to the mirror. Pulling a tube of lipstick from her pocket, she applied just enough.

I've caught him looking at me just like you used to back in high school. What do I say if he should say anything? Ooooh, I'm just too old for this kind of drama."

Giving her hair an extra flip, she whispered, "Steven, please give me a sign."

Stopping just outside the door to his office, she again sucked in a deep breath.

How long had it been since she giggled like this? I feel like a silly school girl.

His smile relaxed her giddiness.

"Please, have a seat." He motioned to a padded chair in front of his desk.

"Is something wrong, sir?"

"Please, for right now, call me George," he said. "And no, nothing's wrong. At least, I hope not."

"Sir?" Her eyebrows drew together. "Oops, sorry. George."

"I have a report here from the security office in reference to vandalism to your vehicle. Apparently, they have done an extensive investigation and have found no evidence as to who did this."

She sucked in a deep breath and blew it out. "I didn't think they would. The officers seemed to think that someone in my apartment building had done it. But, they're all my friends and some of them will be going up with me."

"And you don't suspect any of them at all?"

"No, I absolutely do not."

He closed the folder. "All right then. But, would you promise me something?"

"I'll try."

"I realize the next few days are going to be breathtakingly busy for you, but promise me that you'll make a conscientious effort to observe everyone around you for any signs of jealousy or dislike toward you."

"I'll try."

"Promise."

"Okay, I promise."

"Fine. Thank you."

"You're welcome." Her eyes couldn't hide her excitement.

"You're looking forward to this mission, aren't you?"

"Like you wouldn't believe, sir…George." She giggled. "I've worked so incredibly hard for this and now…" her hands lifted as if her favorite team scored a touchdown. "Here it is."

"Obviously, I won't be going, but I will be in the control room keeping my eye on things. This is a first in many ways. The outcome of this trial mission will set the standard for the first civilian vacation seekers waiting with their tickets in hand."

"Who would ever have dreamed that one day civilians would not only choose this type of vacation, but have the opportunity to fulfill their dream? From the reports I've read, those who are going and the two who will be doing the space walk with us have almost finished their training."

"They are; and they're almost as excited as you."

George walked over to the window with his hands shoved in his pockets, something he rarely did.

"Is something else bothering you, George?" Nicol asked.

He pulled a chair close where he could look into her face. "I'm in a quandary.

I don't know exactly what the protocol is for this."

"For what, sir?"

His eyebrows lifted.

"George," she corrected herself with a slight smile that tugged at one side of her lips that his eyes were glued on.

"Nicol, my duties have been to oversee all the trainees for this mission and weed out the ones who weren't going to pass muster. I think you know that you've surpassed all the others and everyone in command of this mission has every confidence in the world in your ability to make it a go."

A charming blush washed over her face.

"Thank you," she whispered.

"You're aware of the risks associated with this?"

She nodded as her fingers weaved together.

His hand covered hers. "Nicol, I...I...I don't want to lose you." His eyes shimmered.

"Why would that happen, sir?" Her eyebrows drew together.

Clearing his throat, he answered, "It wouldn't and it shouldn't." His hand tightened over hers

Like a frightened fawn, Nicol rose and hurried to the window. Please, Stephen, what do I do?

With the patience of awakened love, George waited.

Long minutes passed before Nicol turned to him. "George, I don't plan on going to the other side of space just yet."

"Excuse me?"

"I apologize," she smiled and wiped her hands down the sides of her slacks. "It was just a conversation I had with my son."

"Your son? But, I thought he was..."

"Yes, well, when I'm home, I usually visit the cemetery and talk to him and my husband."

"Oh, I understand."

"I know, it sounds silly, but it helps."

Standing, he moved close to her. "It's not silly at all." Looking deeply into her eyes, he said, "Promise me you'll stay safe."

Feeling as if her heart was going to jump out of her chest, she rolled in her lips and met his gaze. "I promise, sir."

The kiss was tender. Like a video on fast-forward, the memories sped behind her closed eyes. Feeling her silent sobs, he knew. Love cradled her in his embrace.

In a small cemetery in southeastern Kentucky, a lone miniature rose on Nathan's side of the black granite stone fell from its stem.

CHAPTER 8

Bright orange launch and entry suits had been worn by the crew as they climbed into the orbiter and ran through the launch procedures and practiced the escape procedures.

The time-honored ritual, beginning with the original NASA astronauts, of the card game had been played; the cake had been a beautiful temptation, especially for the ladies; and the crew left the astronaut quarters which were still decorated with stickers from every previous mission.

It was time. Various good luck charms or other special items were stored somewhere on their persons. Nicol's orange-colored New Testament that she had received from a Gideon while she was in high school, matched her launch suit.

Cybil and Dalyn's heart rates rose. Other than the moment George's lips touched hers, Nicol's heart remained calm, even though her lips still seemed to tingle from a not-so-long-ago kiss.

Nestled in the newly refurbished space shuttle, her eyes closed as she silently put herself, the crew, and her parents into the hands of God.

While the world watched with bated breath, Galaxy Adventure's shuttle roared from its platform, thrusting itself upward and outward until it punctured the atmosphere and soared through its orbits.

The reality of finally being in space filled Nicol with an exhilaration that far surpassed anything she had ever experienced in her life so far.

Dalyn's usual perky personality changed to pesky. Already sensitive from Dalyn's barbs, Cybil's patience with Nicol's almost giddy attitude pushed her to the ragged edge.

"Ladies." Alex Herald's voice commanded their attention. "Our objective is to work together, you know, as a team. We're in space, which is a first for most of us; but, we are not novices. We have trained together and what we don't need now is any female cat fights."

"Excuse me?" Resentment sent flames across Cybil's face.

Embarrassment brushed a deep blush across Nicol's cheeks.

"Oh, my word," she said. "Alex, you're correct. I've been acting like an aggravating school girl. I so apologize to everyone."

"Yeah," Dalyn muttered. "Me, too. I hope the last hour hasn't been recorded for posterity." Her giggle brought the sparkle back into her eyes.

"One to add to the books," Cybil said. "God bless America." With a smirk, she swished around to focus on retrieving a all-to-soon snack from the food locker.

Nicol's face continued to burn chasing any words from her mind. Focused on studying each detail of her upcoming space walk on her iPad, her silent prayer for God's help calmed the heat.

Unlike Cybil's silky red hair, Alex's hair, eyebrows, and eyelashes were a burnt orange-red that made his ice blue eyes as striking as ice chips on Santa's cap. Just like Nicol, he gave one hundred and fifty percent. Throughout their training, his competition, although silent, had been as intense as an incensed bull.

Like a ghost, he floated behind her. When his hand touched her shoulder, she jumped.

"Yikes, you startled me," she laughed.

"Cramming for tomorrow's final?" he asked, keeping his hand on her shoulder.

"That's a good way of putting it," she said. "Technically, I'm an astronaut, but my official title is Space Walk Hostess. Being responsible for the lives of civilians out there is heavy. I don't want to forget one jot or tittle."

"Odd choice of words," he said. As if her shoulder suddenly flared red hot, his hand jerked back.

"Just quoting Scripture," she said.

"Oh, yeah," he said. "I remember that from eons ago."

Twisting her head to look at him, she grinned. "Somehow you don't look that old."

"Everything's ready. Best of luck." He floated back to his station.

CHAPTER 9

It was almost time for the evening news; Monica snuggled in the corner of the couch waiting. "Jim, you need to hurry or else you're going to miss it." Her words whooshed through the screen door to reach no listening ears.

Hearing a car approach, she shouted. "Hurry, honey."

In anticipation, she leaned forward to look out the door. "Oh, no, it's the preacher," she muttered. "I don't want to miss the news. Shoot." Shoving herself off the couch she walked to the door.

"Howdy, Preacher Baker, come on it."

"I'm afraid I can't right now, Monica," he said.

She saw it in his eyes; her breath caught.

"Monica, Jim's in the hospital and needs you to come as quickly as you can. I've come for you."

"What?" While the questions begin to pour out, she snatched her purse and pulled the door shut behind her. "What's happened? Did he have an accident? How badly is he hurt?"

After shutting her door, Preacher Baker rushed around to his side and slid in, jerking the car into reverse.

"No, Preacher Baker, please don't tell me…"

"Monica, I found Jim in the cemetery…" Preacher Baker was cut off by her sobs.

"No, no," she sobbed. "Not now. Not today."

"Apparently, he's had a heart attack. I got him to the hospital as quickly as I could and he sent me for you, not wanting you to drive."

"You mean, he's still alive?" Hope charged through her aching chest.

"Yes, he's alive," Preacher Baker said. "The doctors were working on him when I left to get you."

Her hands tented over her mouth; her eyes squeezed shut. Prayers sped from her heart to Heaven.

"Hannah's started the prayer chain, so everyone is praying."

Monica nodded her gratitude. "Oh, how can I tell Nicol?" Fresh tears ran down her face.

"Everyone's been praying for her, too," Preacher Baker said. "Most everybody is glued to their television sets about now. We sure are proud of her."

"Thanks, Preacher Baker," Monica said. "I don't know what we'd do without our church family."

"It's the Lord, Monica," Preacher Baker said as he parked next to the emergency entrance. "He's in control."

Even though Monica agreed whole-heartedly, she ran through the automatic doors of the emergency room almost before they were opened wide enough.

Her purse hung in the crook of her arm as her fingers interlaced over her lips. No! Oh, God, please, no.

Through the spaghetti of wires and tubes, Jim lay white and still. Beeps, hums, and hissing noises filled the room.

Creeping to his side, she reached for his hand that was lying across his stomach.

"Jim?"

His eyes fluttered but failed to open. "Monica." His lips moved but made no sound.

"Jim, I'm here, darling." Her chest ached as she tried to keep calm for his sake. "I'm here."

A smile tugged at the corner of his dry lips. Weighted with the load of drugs, his eyelids slowly rose.

"There you are," Monica's eyes shone into his with her love. Her hand pressed against his cheek. "I'm sorry I wasn't there with you, honey."

His head shook as slow as molasses. "Didn't need to be, darlin'."

One sob escaped; her head nodded. "I'm here now and I won't be leaving."

His eyelids drooped; his head nodded once; he smiled.

The nurse handed Monica a handful of tissues. "He's still with us, Monica. He's just resting a moment."

The doctor stepped into the room. "Monica, I'd like to talk with you."

Out of Jim's earshot, the doctor, a friend who had gone to church with them for years, spelled out all the details. "It's entirely in God's hands, Monica. His heart has suffered irreparable damage. What's amazing is that he's still hanging on. He said he had a message for you before he goes."

"What?" she sobbed.

"I don't know," the doctor said with his arm around her shoulder. "When he could speak, he kept saying, "I have to tell Monica first"."

"Tell me what?" she pulled away and hurried to Jim's bedside.

"Jim?" Her hand caressed his face.

"Monica," his voice was an air-filled whisper. "Need to tell you."

"Get some rest, then we'll talk," she said, bending over to kiss his dry lips.

"No...now."

"Jim, if you have a message for me, God will allow you to deliver it. Please, rest so you'll be stronger. I promise I'll be right here."

His hand rose to cover hers.

Preacher Baker guided her to a chair which had been situated where she could see his face yet allow the emergency room team to tend to their patient.

Preacher Baker knelt on one knee and covered her hands with one of his. "Monica, when I found him, he had collapsed across Nathan's grave."

Monica moaned as sobs shook her shoulders.

"I called 911, then gently rolled him over. His hand was clutching the front of his shirt, but he said "Nathan's waiting for me." He smiled through his pain and went as still as stone. I carried him down to my car and got here just as the ambulance was pulling out."

"Thank you, Preacher Baker," Monica said, wiping her face for what seemed like the hundredth time. "He saw Nathan? Is that possible?"

Preacher Baker lifted his shoulders. "With God, anything's possible." Etched on his face was pain as he slowly stretched himself up, rubbing the side of his knee.

"Nicol," Monica whispered. "She's so excited about her space walk tomorrow. How can I tell her this?"

"Let's just wait," the preacher said. "It's not as if they can drop her in by parachute."

Monica giggled. "Guess you're right about that. I wonder what she would want me to do?"

"Monica?" the nurse touched her arm. "Jim wants you."

As quick as a wink, she was by his side. "Honey, I'm here."

His eyes were opened and exceptionally bright. "Monica, I have something to tell you." His voice was as strong as before he left their home earlier.

Her heart beat thudded in her ears.

His hand gripped hers. "I went to clean the graves. Nathan met me and told me that he's waiting for me and not be afraid because it's beautiful and happy where he is."

Sounding like a wounded cat, Monica moaned. Her uncaught tears dripped on his chest.

"Oh, Nathan," she whispered.

"Darlin, I don't want to leave you, but I think it's my time," Jim said, his grip getting tighter. "We've talked about this, remember?"

"Yes, honey, I remember," she said. "I don't want you to go, but it's okay. Just tell Nathan that Mamaw still loves him." A sob caught in her throat. Her hand began to hurt from Jim's grip.

"Please, don't tell Nici until she gets back," Jim said. His eyes seemed to be on fire. "Promise me."

"I promise, honey," she said, kissing his hot cheek. "I promise."

The monitors were making noises she hadn't heard before. Looking into her husband's eyes, she watched his life ebb.

"Monica?" his voice seemed far away.

"Yes, darling," she said loudly just in case he truly was far away.

"I'll still love you forever." His hand relaxed; his eyes emptied.

Silently, Monica lay across Jim's chest with her face nestled against his neck just under his ear.

With questions they didn't want to ask, the nurses and doctor looked at each other and waited.

Long, pain-filled minutes passed. Monica's head rose; her hands cupped the face she had loved since she was a teenager. "My darling husband, how do I live without you?" Tenderly, her lips touched his.

Straightening her back, her hands covered his. "You're love for me has been so great, it will last until I meet you again."

Tears trickled down the cheeks of all others in the small cubicle.

"Don't forget to give my love to Nathan," she said. "Jim Amburgy, I will love you for eternity."

Turning slowly, she smiled at the team. "Thank you and God bless each of you."

Looking at Preacher Baker, she asked, "Please, I need to go home. I need to see my daughter."

CHAPTER 10

Seldom did Nicol have difficulties sleeping. The last hours before her space walk, had been no different. Despite that, while going through her morning bathroom rituals, eating breakfast, and taking time to read her New Testament and pray, a niggling sensation kept her alert.

Each step of the way, I've felt you, Father. Are you trying to tell me something that I'm just not hearing now?

Dalyn and Cybil gave Nicol hugs. For the first time, Nicol failed to feel their sincerity. "Are you okay?" she asked each of them.

"Of course," Dalyn said. "Just a busy, busy morning."

"Just glad it's you and not me," Cybil said with a fake smile that niggled Nicol once more.

"All right." She sucked in a deep breath and blew it out quickly. "I'm off to see the wizard; the wonderful wizard of space," she sang.

Finally, it was time. Alex, Paul Feltner, and Nicol spent thirty minutes pre-breathing 100 percent oxygen to remove nitrogen from their blood and tissues, then put on their MAGs (Maximum Absorption Garment). They entered the airlock and began donning and attaching each article and piece of their Extravehicular Mobility Unit (EMU).

The pressure in their EMUs was increased to 0.20 above the airlock pressure to make the last check for leaks. The airlock was depressurized and the astronauts were ready to step out of the airlock into the shuttle's cargo bay.

Paul would be using a Manned Maneuvering Unit (MMU), which was a gas-thruster powered chair with a joystick control. With the nitrogen-gas propelled unit fitted on his backpack, the SAFER would help an astronaut return to the shuttle or space station in the event he, or she, would somehow get separated from the spacecraft.

The next scheduled flight of the shuttle would bring the first of the civilian vacationers. Those who would be taking a space walk would be tethered to the space craft for added safety. One of the crew would be using the MMU, the other and Nicol would maneuver independently from the spacecraft, keeping close to the civilians. For her maiden sashay through space, Nicol would remain tethered.

Feeling like a child on her first carnival ride, Nicol had to control her urge to giggle and summersault herself out into space. Even in the confines of her EMU, she felt as if she were free to discover every inch her new playground.

Following their orders, Alex stayed close to Nicol as they practiced their mobility, and inspected the cargo unit, the mechanical arm that would be used to move equipment around in space, and the heat shield tiles.

Paul re-checked Nicol's tether before boarding his MMU. An accidental bump into the space craft could be disastrous, not only for the spacewalkers, but for the shuttle and all on board.

Nicol's adrenalin rush had long passed and she was beginning to feel the draining effects of movement and working in the EMU. Only an hour to go; I will not give up.

Alex's voice caused her to blink and mentally shake off her fatigue.

"I'm going to check some tiles on the other side while you finish here. Don't run away." Before she could respond, he was out of sight.

"Sure thing; I'm almost done here." Reporting to the commander of the shuttle that the inspection of the tiles was finished, Nicol began to relax. The knowledge that the heat tiles, at least on her side of the spacecraft were safe, gave her peace of mind and pride in the fact that she had accomplished her mission.

While she waited for Alex, she turned away from the shuttle to revel in heavenly grandeur that was wrapped around her making her feel like a tiny white speck. The sheer depth of space mirrored the awesome depth of its beauty. "Amazing," she breathed.

"Repeat that, ma'am," the commander asked.

"I apologize, sir," she said. "I was expressing my awe of this universe."

"Affirmative, ma'am."

This deep in space and it's still as deep, dark, and beautiful as if I were lying on the beach at midnight, staring up at your stars. God, you are an awesome architect. To know that someday I'll have the ability to inspect every nook and cranny of your creation without the need for this space suit, is more than my mind can take in.

"Nathan, even out here, you're still on the other side of space. Sure wish I could stop by for a visit," she whispered. Silence screamed through her Communications Carrier Assembly (CCA). Still checking tiles on the opposite side of the shuttle, Alex was nowhere to be seen. On his MMU, Paul powered toward her.

Like a snake in slow motion, her tether writhed along with her. Panic invaded the confines of her spacesuit. Emergency life support procedures kicked in, just as they were designed to do.

"No, no, no..." she whispered as the separation between herself and the space shuttle grew far too quickly and far too large for Paul to ever reach her.

"Mom, I'm sorry." Her eyes closed; blackness enveloped her as her body relaxed inside the suit that was designed to save her life.

Chaos filled the training center's control room until everyone pulled themselves into rescue mode. The arms of George Surface's chair bent inward as his body tightened. "No!" his mind screamed.

Sandra, and Barbara watched and listened in shocked silence. Jaylee leaned back in her chair.

Helping each other as they rushed through the process of re-entry into the cargo bay, air lock, and the space shuttle itself, Paul's shoulders shook with sobs. Alex, always in control no matter what, rushed forward to give his full report and find out where they were in the recovery effort.

Sitting in his security vehicle listening to the news, Duane Embree's coffee cup cluttered to the driver's side carpet and across his shoes. "No! No, go get her!" His voice thundered against the rolled-up windows.

Beating his fists against the steering wheel, he swore before the only One listening. "When I find whoever did this, they'll die wishing for a black hole in space to hide in, so help me God."

Inside the shuttle, Dalyn and Cybil remained motionless, watching and listening. Shock seemed to have ripped away their abilities to act or react. Observing them closely, the commander made mental notes he would examine later.

Family, church members, and neighbors milled inside Monica's home. Food covered the table and countertops as preparations were made for Jim's funeral.

"No," Monica said. "No," she shouted. "No!" Her scream splashed pain on all those standing in the house.

"What?" echoed throughout the room as everyone crowded around Monica.

"Move, I can't see," she shouted.

All eyes became glued on the television as news with pictures flashed across the wide screen.

"No," echoed across the rooms.

"No, God, this is too much." Monica shoved herself off the couch and grabbed at the TV screen, trying to catch the picture of her daughter as she drifted out of camera range.

Julia Baker, the preacher's wife, wrapped her arm around Monica's waist.

"No." Monica shoved her arm away. "This is too much." She swung her arm outward and toward the door. "Please, I need to be alone."

Bewildered and saddened beyond words, everyone slowly filtered out of her home. Most tried to give Monica warm, supportive hugs as they were leaving, but she stood stiff and cold.

Preacher Baker and Julia were the last. "Monica," he began.

"No, you, too."

The crash of the television screen against the floor was heard by no one but Monica, whose hands smarted from yanking on it so hard. The usual soft beauty of her face was frozen in a hard smirk as she slammed her bedroom door so hard the house shook. Grabbing the folded quilt from the foot of the bed, she jerked it over her entire body and head.

"Monica?" The voice was too full of compassion to not know who was speaking.

"No! Especially, You. No."

Stationing unseen guardians in the four corners of the room, He waited.

One angry tear found its way out of her squeezed eye lids, leading the flood of thousands.

With a nod to the guardians, He smiled.

In the small cemetery on the side of the emerald, green mountain, every tiny rosebud on the bush next to Nathan's stone burst open in deep fiery red, like Moses' burning bush.

CHAPTER 11

Tranquility, like she'd never experienced before, nor could she explain, pervaded the depth of her soul. Her feet were firmly on some type of soil. Someone stood behind and over her. Those hands! And those horrible scars! The hands rested on each side of her helmet. Slowly, the helmet rose and disappeared along with her space suit. A gown made of fabric with the softness of flaxen mink covered her.

Filling her lungs with the sweetest air she had ever encountered, she wondered what it was. Perfection.

"Oh." She looked into his eyes; no longer a little child, yet not a grown man. Age no longer mattered.

"Nathan," she breathed.

"Hi, Mommy." His arms encircled her neck. "Jesus said you were coming for a visit."

"Jesus?" She pulled back to hold his face in her hands. One crystal tear rolled down her cheek.

"Uh huh, this is where He lives," he bubbled. "Come on, Dad and I get to show you around."

There was no sun, or need for one. Light infused everything. How could it be explained? Splendor beyond description

One more crystal tear rolled down the opposite cheek as she rushed into Stephen's waiting arms.

"You said you might stop in for a visit, and here you are," Stephen said.

"We have another surprise for you," he said as the family of three walked hand in hand.

"Daddy?" There was no need for tears.

Jim winked at her. "Hi, darlin'."

With Nathan leading the way, the family of four began walking. Shimmering like crystal, yet with an iridescence of more colors Nicol knew existed, this new world was what she had yearned for longer than she even realized she was yearning.

How could it be explained? Only perfection.

"Mom?" she asked.

"Not yet," Jim replied. "I've been keeping an eye on her mansion's construction. You know, letting them know what she likes and doesn't like."

Their laughter filled the air like music. On a hillside that overlooked more beauty than Nicol could comprehend, the family of four sat on grass like shimmering green glass but softer than badger's fur. Only God's imagination could sprinkle this world with the multitudinous variety and colors of flowers.

Any of Nicol's pre-notions of what Heaven would be were far surpassed by the supernal beauty fanned out around them. Yet, it seemed as if a gossamer veil shielded most of what Nicol yearned to see.

"Dad, how long have you been here?" she asked.

"There is no time here, darlin'," he said. "But, it was the day you thundered into space. It was time for me to join my grandson and son-in-law."

"You've done well, Nicol," Stephen said. "I've been proud of you and your accomplishments."

"You know?"

"There are certain things about our loved ones that we're allowed to see," he said.

"Wow," she whispered.

"And Mom," Nathan said with his arm around her shoulders. "I'm okay. You don't have to worry about me anymore."

"Oh, sweetie," she said. "I've known that you're okay. I've just had a most difficult time missing you."

"The next time you come, we'll get to show you everything. You just won't believe it," Nathan gushed.

"Next time?" Nicol's eyebrows shot up.

"This is just a visit, darlin'," Jim said. "Your mansion isn't even close to being finished."

"No," she gasped. "No, I can't leave you."

"Jesus told us that when He chose you for a visit, it was because He has a job for you when you go back," Nathan said.

"No," she whispered.

"But just think, Mom, if you do the job He has for you, many more people will be able to come here."

Looking into Stephen's eyes, she knew.

Standing to gaze all around her, she realized the veil was moving closer.

She took his hands. "Nathan, my son, it has given me the only peace I've had just knowing that Jesus himself was watching over you. I couldn't pay a babysitter enough for that kind of daycare."

In a boy-man voice, Nathan laughed

Reaching for Stephen's hands, they stood facing each other. "And you, the love of my life," she said. "There has been nothing to fill the Stephen-void in my heart."

"I know," he said. "Here." He placed a miniature rose in the palm of her hand. In his fingers it looked like iridescent crystal. In the palm of her hand, the petals were as soft as velvet and the color of king's purple. Along the edges of each tiny petal glittered the purest gold she had ever seen.

"I could never find a purple rose before."

"A purple rose," she murmured. "Oh, Stephen, thank you."

Looking into her eyes, he said, "Nicol, you have my blessing when it's time."

Dropping her eyes to her purple rose, she nodded.

"Will I know who?"

"You'll know." His finger lifted her face. "Watch the signs."

Their hug sealed his blessing.

Turning to her father, she said, "And Daddy, since I know you're here and you're okay, I'll be able to help mom."

"Thanks, darlin'," he said. "I knew you would."

His eyes focused above her head, Stephen nodded. Looking into her eyes, he said, "It's time, sweetheart."

No tears, no sadness, no dread followed them to the designated spot. Nicol turned to face her family. With closed eyes, she held Nathan as if to soak him into her heart.

"I love you, Mom."

She nodded.

Stephen held her face in his hands. "Remember my blessing." He hugged her to him.

"Daddy," she said as she held his hands.

"I love you, darlin'," he said.

In the snap of a heartbeat, she was in her spacesuit. She whispered, "I will love you forever."

In unison, they called, "God be with you until we see you again."

He stood in front of her with the helmet held in his scared hands.

"Jesus!" Joy sprang into her eyes. The urge to fall to her knees was halted by the touch of his hands. His eyes, filled with love and peace that far surpassed the deepness and purity of Crater Lake's water, reflected her image. All fears and sadness were doused in the depth of him.

"Nicol, you have been given a gift; a gift to share. Use it wisely. The task will be daunting, but remember that I will be with you and will never leave you or forsake you."

She nodded. As his hands placed the helmet on her head, her gloved hands touched the scars. Each beat of his heart pulsed through the thickness of the gloves and into her helmet. "Thank you," she whispered.

He smiled.

"Wait! My rose," she called.

"You'll find what you need." A tiny spot of warmth seeped through the breast pocket of what she liked to call her long underwear that was her first garment donned before she was dressed in her spacesuit. Just as His brilliance began to fade, Nicol was aware of His protecting presence beside her. In a heartbeat, blackness enveloped her.

CHAPTER 12

Dalyn and Cybil strapped themselves in their seats an hour after Nicol disappeared into the ink well of space. As if in a wide-eyed coma, neither spoke, neither responded in any way.

Alex and Paul returned to the opened cargo bay as the shuttle neared the end of its first orbit since losing one of their own. Each searched the ocean of blackness for the possibility of espying a white space suit within snagging distance.

With trillions of planets and tons of space debris, space nonetheless remained black and empty as a desert well. Remaining outside for an hour, just in case, the futility of their search finally dragged them inside.

Stripped from his EVA, Paul immediately wrapped himself into his sleeping unit. Thoughts of Nicol made his body refuse to receive warmth. Each breath was held as if it were his last. His supply of tears had been used up; his eyes burned as if on fire.

Alex floated to the command center of the shuttle. No one asked questions; everyone knew. They had watched her float away. The possibility of finding her was as likely as finding a diamond in an avalanche.

Every available resource, proven or unproven, was put into operation from the space center. Eye sockets ached from searching each infinitesimal dot on each of the monitors and screens in the command center.

"This is it, folks. Ninety minutes and no sightings. We're the experts; any suggestions?"

"Please, sir, one more orbit," George said. "The EVA was redesigned for emergencies such as this. We can't give up now."

"That's affirmative, sir." The consensus was overwhelming.

"One more orbit, then we abort the rescue mission."

No! Never. Nicol has to come back to us—alive. George pushed from his chair and excused himself.

Immediately after receiving the news of Nicol's loss, Duane Embree raced to security headquarters like a bat out of a hot cave. Once inside, he demanded a meeting with all heads of security.

An hour passed while he filled them in on the details of the vandalism to Nicol's Mustang and all of the notes he had taken for his report. Officer Embree knew about the incident in the gym; he knew about the possibility of a jealousy-driven attempt on Nicol's life from one of the other females on board the shuttle. There were other facts Officer Embree was not aware of.

As the shuttle began her second orbit, an intense investigation was not only begun, but was growing like a category five tornado. Officer Embree would make certain that someone would pay for the deadly results.

Jim and Monica's small Kentucky church was filled with friends, family, and curiosity seekers. Like a stiff-backed schoolmarm, Monica waited dry-eyed on the front pew.

Preacher Baker's words of comfort were followed by soft music. Almost everyone in the church filed by for their last look at the earthly body of Jim Amburgy. Those who stopped to hug Monica felt as if her body was the one that was dead.

Her stone cold emotions stiffened her body, her face, her jaws. Monica was known as the sweetest, kindest and most generous woman in the community. Since the moment Nicol drifted into the dark ocean of space, the Monica everyone knew ceased to exist.

The American flag covering Jim's casket was folded. The youngest member of the local American Legion honor guard played a haunting rendition of taps that echoed between the mountains.

The lone show of emotion from Monica were twin tears that rolled down her cheeks as the last whisper of taps floated over Jim's casket. Against everyone's wishes, she stood beside his silver casket as it was lowered into the ground just inches away from their grandson.

Nathan, your mommy won't even get to sleep beside you. She's lost up there in the dark. Mamaw is so sorry.

Darkness was creeping down the mountainside before Monica moved. Preacher Baker and Julia waited beside their vehicle, the last one in the parking lot. The grave closers had gathered their shovels and rakes and had driven away.

Alone, Monica melted. On her knees beside the mound of fresh dirt, she placed one hand on top of the grave. "I'm assuming you and Nicol are together. For that I am thankful. But, Jim, this is just too much. First Nathan, now you and Nicol at the same time. It's too much." Dammed up tears spilled down her face, falling onto the grave. "You were my rock; what do I do now?"

Feeling hands on her elbows, she slowly stood, stooped like an elderly woman.

Emotionally and physically drained, she allowed herself to be guided to the path leading down to the parking lot.

Halfway there, she stopped when she saw the preacher and his wife waiting, looking up at her. Jerking around, she saw emptiness.

Like a child, she dropped onto her bottom, folding her arms across her knees, and cried as if she would never stop.

Julia started to run toward her when her husband caught her arm. "Give her a minute, honey."

"But..."

"Give her time." He put his arm around his wife as they walked slowly to the beginning of the path.

CHAPTER 13

"One more orbit before we abort." Mission control's order seemed to hang in a no-gravity environment full of constant movement.

Alex's loud retort, "Are they insane? Don't they have any notion how futile this is. She's gone!" was followed by a loud expletive.

Jonathan Armstrong, the shuttle's commander, twisted around. "That, sir, will not be tolerated on my ship. Understood?" His voice thundered through the shuttle.

"Yes, sir," Alex said. "I apologize, sir." He drifted to his seat and belted himself in. Struggling to keep his face blank as an erased blackboard, inside he was sulking like an adolescent child.

"Commander Armstrong, advise your crew to keep a sharp lookout throughout the next ninety minutes."

"Yes, sir." Switching on all inboard speakers, Jonathan relayed the orders. "We have ninety minutes to find our lost astronaut. Ladies, you have a job to do, do it. Paul, Alex, suit up and step outside. This is it; we will not go home without her."

There was never any question about Jonathan's orders even though his voice was soft. But today there was no mistaking his determination to get the job done.

Paul's burning eyes blinked as if an army of gnats were trying to invade his eyelids. Peeling himself from his sleeping bag, he moved as quickly as possible to the air lock.

I'll search as far out as possible with my MMU. If it runs out of nitrogen-gas and I drift off too, so be it. At least she won't be alone.

With help from Dalyn, Cybil, and each other, the men soon were suited up and ready. Alex didn't miss the haunted look in and around Paul's eyes.

What is with all these people? These things happen in the space program. No one told me she was some kind of goddess. His ugly smirk was hidden behind his visor.

Jaylee and Cybil squinted at the monitors. The commander and his co-pilot watched out the windows and their monitors. Moving with the speed of the shuttle, Paul nevertheless shot out occasionally to check a sighting, only to be chased back by disappointment. Alex made continual loops around the shuttle; his eyes ached from straining at what he considered a space gnat.

"What is that?" George shouted, jumping to his feet.

Faces closed in on monitors; tension in the command center became intense.

"I see something!" Paul shouted. A surge of nitrogen-gas shot him away from the shuttle.

"Confirm first, Paul," Jonathan shouted into his mic.

"It's her; I know it's her," Paul's response began to fade.

"Paul, wait!" Alex shouted.

"Oh, God, let it be; let her be alive." George's whisper was lost in the sudden explosion of excited chaos in the command center.

Against every scientific fact known to the space industry, a tiny white speck dragging a swishing tether moved toward the space shuttle, not in the opposite direction.

His vision squiggly from tears, Paul powered his MMU in her direction. Finally able to grasp the tether, he slowed his speed as he maneuvered back to the shuttle. Taking no chances of damaging the tether and losing her again or bumping into her EVA and possibly tearing a death hole in it, he moved toward the cargo bay.

Alex waited, ready to grasp Nicol and maneuver her into the airlock. Even though she remained in the blackness of unconsciousness, Nicol felt the softness of warmth in a tiny spot on her chest.

Everyone on board gathered around to lift her inside and rush her to sick bay.

With the tenderness of a new mother clothing her baby, Dalyn removed the helmet. After the struggle of removing the spacesuit from an inert body, hands prepared to lift her into sick bay.

"Wait!" squealed Cybil. "She moved."

"Are you insane?" Alex barked as he began to lift.

Nicol's hand touched his arm and squeezed.

No one moved.

"Nicol?" Alex whispered.

The rush to get her into sickbay halted as her crew members watched her chest rise, filling with oxygen. Her eyelashes began to move; her grip on Alex's arm tightened.

Dark, curled lashes lifted, revealing the deepness of blue in eyes that focused on Alex's.

A trembling began deep in his core as fear began to birth. Unable to suck in a breath so he could lift her, his arms began to tremble. His knees knocking, a sensation he'd never experienced before, kept him from straightening his body.

"Alex," Nicol whispered.

Everyone froze.

"I'm okay." Her smile spoke life into the crew.

As if their team had just made a touchdown, their whoops and whistles filled the belly of the shuttle.

Alex's ruddy cheeks pulled back into as much of a smile as his shaking body could muster. Nicol's eyes remained locked on his.

"Alex," she whispered. Her eyes squinted, willing him to understand. "I am really okay."

The surge of energy from her hand to his arm was warm and tingly. Staring into the eyes he couldn't turn away from, tears began to form. Feeling like a deflating balloon, Alex's knees buckled. Pulling her hand to his tear washed cheek, he nodded.

"Would someone help me up?" Nicol asked.

Pushing himself around Alex, Paul scooped Nicol into his arms;

with the help of Dalyn he placed her in the seat behind the captain's and belted her in.

Commander Armstrong bent to kiss the top of Nicol's head on his way to his pilot's chair. "Welcome back, Nicol. We're heading home."

Jonathan relayed the welcomed good news to mission control; mission control in turn relayed information that put the shuttle within minutes of re-entry.

"Prepare for re-entry," he advised his crew.

Sitting across from each other, Dalyn and Cybil held hands. Paul took Alex's seat as if it were his own to keep watch on Nicol.

Trying to decipher the emotions swirling inside him like a white and black tornado, Alex slouched inside his seat harness

Commander Armstrong flipped a special switch. "Yes, sir."

Silently listening, he nodded. "Affirmative, sir. Yes, I understand."

The strength of his anger could have torn the switch from the board. His jaws clinched to the point of popping. Re-entry details were happening far too quickly for him to remain distracted by that anger.

The RCS thrusters were fired; the orbiter was now in tail-first position. The crew fired the OMS engines to slow the orbit for the fall back to earth. Twenty-five minutes until the shuttle would reach the upper atmosphere.

Those twenty-five minutes were filled with activities that would reposition the shuttle for a safe, uneventful re-entry. The RCS thrusters would be fired again to pitch the orbiter over about forty degrees so that the bottom would face the atmosphere. Leftover fuel would be burned to protect against an explosion and/or fire.

The friction, built up from heat as the orbiter hits air molecules at 17,000 miles per hour, could easily cause an explosion or fire which would cause a catastrophe such as the Columbia in 2003.

Everything was going as it should; Commander Armstrong steepened the angle of descent to minus twenty degrees and pulled up the nose. The landing gear was deployed and the commander braked the orbiter and the speed brake on the vertical tail opened up. A parachute deployed and the orbiter finally came to a stop midway to the three-quarters of the way down the runway.

"Dalyn."

"Nicol…" On her knees she held Nicol's hands.

"I'll see you inside, sweetie."

Dalyn tripped on nothing other than her nerves. The commander caught her before she tumbled into the floor. With a nervous giggle, she shook his hand. "Thank you, sir." Her vehicle followed Cybil's as they paraded to the waiting buildings.

"Can you walk, Nicol?" Commander Armstrong asked, standing beside her seat.

"I think so." Gingerly, she pushed herself to her feet.

"I thought you might want to show the world that you are indeed okay." Jonathan took her elbow and guided her forward. Just outside of camera range, he stopped. "You will be debriefed to the nth, you know that, right?"

Nodding, she smiled. "Yes, sir. I certainly know that."

"We haven't had time to talk, but in time I certainly would like to hear whatever you can remember."

"Sir, they may lock me in a loony bin somewhere when I tell them about my space walk, but take my word for it, it happened. And, sir, I will share every minute with you. You waited for me. Thank you." Her arms stretched around his neck.

Standing just inside the door, within camera range, Commander Armstrong saluted as the world watched a miracle walk out the door and down the ramp into the waiting hands of emergency personnel.

The pilot was followed by the commander into their waiting emergency vehicles. The shuttle, inside and out, would have an inspection like no other. Answers would be found.

CHAPTER 14

Nicol's debriefing was to begin immediately following her medical exam. Like an expectant new father, George paced the hall.

"Ms. Nolan," the doctor began.

"Nicol, please."

"Nicol," he continued. "We won't have final results until lab analysis is completed. The thing is, I see nothing out of the ordinary. You are in perfect health."

"Yes, sir. I could have told you that and saved the government oodles of money." Her smile seemed to brighten the room like the doctor's examination lamp.

"You do understand why we're baffled here, correct?" he asked, fiddling with his stethoscope.

"Yes, sir, I do understand," Nicol said. "There is a very real explanation that most everyone out there waiting will not believe. I will speak with George Surface first and then I will share with those who think they need to know."

The doctor's eyebrows drew together. "Will I ever be given this miracle's explanation?"

"Oh, yes, doctor." Her smile returned. "I promise you'll know."

"Good enough." He patted her shoulder. "You go ahead and get dressed. I'll pass your request on to George Surface."

"Thank you, doctor."

CHAPTER 15

Whisked down the hallway and out of the medical facility into the waiting vehicle made Nicol's head swim. Surrounded by human shields and with George Surface beside her no one could see her, nor could she see over or around her guardians.

"Now I know how the president of the United States feels," she said when she and George were sequestered in the back of the long black van with darkened windows.

"Speaking of the president," George said. "He ordered a full investigation of your accident. One of the base's security guards had already given information that put the investigation in full gear before the president was notified."

"Who was that and how did he know anything?" Nicol asked.

"His name is Duane Embree. He worked the vandalism case involving your car."

"Yes, that's right," Nicol said. "You mean that was related to what happened up there?"

"Yes, we believe so."

"Are you telling me that what happened up there was not accidental?" Nicol's hand covered her heart.

"It was no accident."

Turning her head, she looked out the window.

"George…"

"Nicol..."

Their words collided.

"Go ahead," she said.

"No, ma'am. Ladies first."

"That's too painful to think about, so I need to tell you about what happened up there."

"You mean, you know?"

"No, not that," she said. "What happened while I was gone away from the ship."

"You mean you remember it? It was my understanding..."

"Actually, George, you might not understand it."

"We're scheduled to meet with the officials and the investigators for your de-briefing."

"No, George." Her eyes begged as she grabbed his hand. "Please, I have to tell you what happened. Please?"

His eyebrows pulled together. "Let me see what I can do." He dug his cell phone from his jacket pocket.

For fifteen minutes they had been parked in front of the building that housed his office and auditorium where each of the shuttle crew were being questioned. The guards were lined up, waiting.

"Yes, sir, I understand. Thank you, sir," George said. Snapping his cell phone shut, he turned with a smile. "They've given you until 0800 tomorrow. The other interviews are still in progress anyway."

"Thank you," she said. "Come on, let's get to your office before I burst with my adventure."

"Adventure?"

"Like I said, you won't believe it."

Shielded inside the human wall with weapons, Nicol and George were rushed inside the building.

CHAPTER 16

With his hands clasped behind his back, George stood looking out his office window. The stillness of catacombs filled the room. With her ankles crossed and her hands pressed together like a nun in prayer, Nicol waited.

Like the footsteps of a ghost, Nicol's words glided to George's ears. "You don't believe me." Devastation deafened her. When his hands touched her knees, her feet jerked apart, kicking him in the thigh.

"Oh," she cried, trying to shove her chair backward. "Oh, I'm so sorry. I didn't..."

To calm her moment of panic, George's arms gathered her to him. "Sh-h-h-h."

"I'm so sorry." Her plea was smothered against his shoulder.

"Sh-h-h-h," he whispered. "Nicol, you have no idea."

Sniffling, she pulled back slightly. "No idea? What do you mean?" Looking into his eyes, she saw how deep this moment was for him.

Sitting back on his heels, he let his hands slide down her arms, grasping her hands in his. "Almost since the moment I met you, I've considered you to be an angel. As time passed, you have become my angel. And now, you're a true angel. You've been there."

"George," she whispered. Stephen gave me his blessing."

"Blessing? What kind of blessing?"

"This! Us!"

"He knows about us?"

She nodded.

Gently pulling her from her chair, he gathered her close.

"So, you believe me?" Her hands caressed the sides of his face.

"Of course, I believe you. Your face! It glows like Moses' when he came off the mountain."

Both slowly sat down still holding hands.

"I saw Jesus. I saw his hands; they still have scars. He removed my helmet when I first got there and put it back on before sending me back."

Suddenly, her hand slapped her chest where her uniform pocket had been. "My rose!"

Almost knocking his chair over, George rushed to his desk, pulling out the center drawer.

"What?" Nicol asked.

"Is this what you're looking for?" Holding out a small plastic pouch that was sealed with red evidence tape, he hurried back to her. Inside was what appeared to be some type of flattened rock.

"My rose petal. Oh, Stephen." Holding the package to her chest, she cried like a lost child who had been found. One purple petal of your love.

"No one knew what this was, so the doctor gave it to me," George said.

Still holding the pouch against her heart, covered by both hands, Nicol scooted back in her chair. George pulled his chair close where he could face her.

"You've never been to my home in Kentucky, but I have always loved miniature roses. I don't know if they even exist, but I always wanted a purple rose and Stephen, my husband, was always on a quest to find one for me. Never finding one, he would buy me the deepest colored red he could find.

In Heaven, there were more flowers than I thought existed—and the colors were breathtaking. Stephen gave me this tiny purple rose with edges etched in gold. Look." She opened the pouch and poured the petal into the palm of her hand.

George's hands gripped the arms of his chair as he watched the transformation of what he thought was a rock into an iridescent purple rose petal rimmed in gold.

"Nicol," he gasped.

"It's okay," she said, reaching her hand toward him. "Here, you can hold it."

Pouring the petal into George's hand, it was Nicol's turn to gasp. The second the tiny petal left her flesh and touched his, it returned to what looked like a tiny dead rock.

Placing the petal back in her hand, George smiled as the purple and gold petal sparkled.

Folding her fingers over the petal, she held her treasure from Heaven against her heart.

"Touching you right now, and holding your petal from Heaven, is as close as I'll ever be to Heaven," he said.

"Ever?"

"Until I go there myself." George's laugh brought relief to her face. "I have a special thank you for a young man waiting for you up there."

"Two young men," she corrected.

"I stand corrected, ma'am," George said. Sliding back in his chair, he sucked in a deep breath, slowly blowing it out. "Now, how much of this do we share with that committee down the hall?"

"I think it's a given that they will think my brain lacked oxygen long enough to cause me to hallucinate." Worry darkened her eyes.

"The truth they are trying to ferret out is who is responsible for losing you and why." He paused to smile. "Whatever you experienced out there will only add color to a very serious issue: sabotage of the new space venture and attempted murder."

"Oh, my." Nicol leaned back in her chair, still holding her fist-enclosed petal against her heart. "They think someone actually tried to kill me?"

"I'm afraid someone did just that."

Closing her eyes, Nicol remained silent for several minutes. George waited.

Finally, she opened her eyes and shook her head. George smiled as the purple petal edged in gold sparkled in her hand.

"No, I cannot accept that. No one could hate me that much, George. Please tell me that no one could hate me that much."

"Personally, I believe it was more a case of jealousy that got out of hand. It's possible that whoever is responsible, didn't think past unhooking your tether, thinking you would be saved before you drifted too far."

"This is serious, George," she said. "This can't be allowed to set back this space program any further. How can I keep that from happening?"

"My first instinct is to advise you to tell them you don't remember anything," George said.

"I can't lie."

"I know you can't," he said. "So, you'll have to tell them the truth and see what they do with it."

"I have proof, so they'll have to believe me."

He fisted his hand around hers that encased the rose petal. "No."

"What?" her eyes widened. "Why?"

"They'll insist on testing it to make sure it's not space debris that will contaminate everyone."

"No," she whispered. "They'll kill it." Her eyes closed as tears seeped through her long, curled lashes.

Drawing in a deep ragged breath, she opened her eyes and smiled. "George, for years I've had to trust God; He's all I've had. Jesus sent this back with me. I will tell the truth; I will not surrender my treasure from Stephen. God will protect it; I will trust Him."

Both jumped when sharp knocks on the door resounded through the room.

"Well, here goes. Say a prayer for me." She slipped the pouch into her pocket and stood up.

"Ms. Nolan, please follow me," the first guard said when George opened the door.

Accompanying her to the interrogation room, George was stopped at the door.

"Sorry, sir, this is far as you go." Nodding, he stepped back.

Like a school girl, she glanced over her shoulder and gave him a wink. He smiled and hurried back to his office. Standing at his window, he put her in the safest hands he knew of.

CHAPTER 17

Battleship gray walls wrapped around two long tables that faced each other. Nicol was seated in the single chair at the first table. Two female and two male officers sat facing her with stiff veneers of old western hanging judges.

Swallowing her fear, Nicol pressed in her lips and rolled them back into a beautiful smile. "Good afternoon, ladies and gentlemen."

Caught off guard by her pleasant demeanor, the interrogators squirmed in their seats and nodded towards her with faux smiles.

"Good afternoon, Ms. Nolan," the lead interrogator, Officer Sandlin said. "We fully understand that you have not been given the opportunity to rest and recuperate from your ordeal, but we need to ascertain certain facts while they are still fresh in everyone's mind."

"Sir," Nicol interrupted. "If I may, I have a special request before you begin."

Startled looks were exchanged along the long table facing her.

"And what would that be?"

"Sir, I fully intend to give you as many facts about what you call my ordeal, but before I begin, I would like to request that all recorders and all video devices be turned off. When I am finished telling you everything I remember, you can decide what to do with that information. At that point, if you insist on recording the proceedings, I will bow to your wishes."

"That is highly irregular, Ms. Nolan," he said. "To ascertain the facts and bring the guilty party to justice, we have to have recorded evidence."

"I understand that, sir," Nicol said. "If you would please allow me to share my story, then I hope you will understand why I make this request. And I'd like to add, sir, if this request is not granted, I'm not certain how much I can truly remember from my ordeal."

Silence clawed at the gray walls.

"Ma'am, we in no way suspect that you are guilty of wrong doing."

"That's good to hear, sir," Nicol said with her eyes sparkling. "My request still stands."

Officer Sandlin turned toward his panel. The female officer with the grey-streaked hair, Officer Kimmel slid a paper to him. What's the harm?

Each nodded in agreement.

After each camera and recording device had been turned off and the guards excused, Nicol's fingernails tapped the table in anticipation.

"All right, Ms. Nolan, you have the floor."

"Thank you, sir. Please allow me to finish, then I will answer any questions you have."

Each of the panel nodded.

In the space of only forty-five minutes, Nicol had shared her short life with her husband and son and the details of her even shorter visit with her husband and son on the other side of space. With her hands clinched in her lap and struggling to control tears that threatened to gather like a spring rain. Officer Kimmel listened intently. Officer Sandlin dropped his head into his hands, rubbing his forehead; he fought to honor her request to finish her story before questioning the ridiculous narrative he was listening to. The other male officer, Mr. Wever, folded his arms across his chest and pursed his lips, but his eyes watched the truth unfold before him. The remaining officer, Miss Blackwell, a younger, blond-haired female, remained impassive with her hands resting on the arms of her chair.

"I have one thing to show you, then I will answer any questions you have." Nicol quietly pushed back her chair and reached into her pocket. "This is proof that I have been there and have returned."

Pulling the pouch from her pocket, she slid out the petal. Holding out her hand, the purple petal edged in gold shimmered in her palm.

Tears slipped down Officer Kimmel's cheeks; Mr. Wever straightened in his chair; Officer Sandlin's mouth opened but only silence passed his lips.

"And what is this supposed to prove?" Miss Blackwell asked.

"This." Nicol slid the petal from her palm into Miss Blackwell's. Before their eyes, the shimmering petal faded to a piece of dead stone.

Officer Kimmel's hands tented over her mouth.

"How did you do that?" Miss Blackwell gasped. As if it were a hot coal, she dropped the petal back into Nicol's hand.

"I did nothing, ma'am."

As if touching the item would contaminate him, Mr. Wever leaned back in his chair.

"May I?" Officer Sandlin asked, holding out his hand.

In the blink of an eye, the petal died in his hand. Daring to finger it, he held it up to the light, turning and twisting it for his complete inspection. As gentle as handing over a bubble, he placed the petal into the palm of Nicol's hand.

Immediately, the tiny petal burst to life, shimmering like a polished diamond.

"May I," Officer Kimmel asked in a quiet, awe-filled voice.

The dead-like stone lay in her hand. A sob escaped her constricted throat. "It's true. You've been there." Her fingers closed around the petal as if she were trying to feel the touch of Heaven.

"Yes, ma'am. I've been there." Nicol said, holding out her hand for her piece of Heaven.

"Thank you," Officer Kimmel whispered.

"Uh, thank you Ms. Nolan," Officer Sandlin said. "Obviously, something special happened somewhere along the line, but we do have a few questions now, if you don't mind. Please turn on all recorders."

"Yes, sir," Nicol said, sitting with her rose petal held between her hands.

"It is our job here to find out who is responsible for your tether being unhooked from the shuttle and consequently almost losing you and putting the new space program in grave jeopardy."

"Sir, I honestly do not have any idea who could have been responsible. It is my hope that it could very easily have been a total accident."

"Ms. Nolan, something like a tether being unhooked would never be accidental."

"If someone is responsible, sir, I cannot even dare guess who that might be."

"Your vehicle was vandalized some weeks before, is that correct?"

"Yes, sir, I did," Nicol answered. "But, as the weeks passed, I was never informed by the security department as to who could have done the damage."

"Are you telling us that you were not aware of anyone having hard feelings toward you, jealousy, or any outward desire to cause you harm?" Miss Blackwell asked.

"Ma'am, I don't have the time or the desire to find out if someone is a bit jealous of me. I was a trainee, just like everyone else. I was of the opinion that we were more or less a team."

"For someone to deliberately try to get rid of you, Ms. Nolan, it should have been obvious to you." Miss Blackwell's sneer matched her tone.

"The one thing that is of grave concern to me is that this new space program will be damaged beyond repair if this entire episode is not handled in such a way so that if anyone is responsible, they can be dealt with quietly and we can continue in this great endeavor," Nicol said. "You can sneer at me for what I've just shared with you. You can accuse me of covering up for whomever, but the space program is what's at stake here and I will do whatever is in my power to protect it and see that it continues far into our future."

Caught off guard, for the second time, by Nicol's forceful statement, each of the panel sat staring at her as if they were suddenly seeing a stranger in front of them.

Clearing his throat, Officer Sandlin, said, "So, you're suggesting that we sweep this incident under the rug and push forward?"

"No, sir," she answered. "What I'm saying is that if someone did indeed unhook my tether, it had to be for the expressed purpose of damaging this space program. Why give them the satisfaction?"

"And how do you suggest we settle this matter, Ms. Nolan?" Miss. Blackwell snapped.

For the first time since drifting away from the space shuttle, Nicol spit-fire protection of the space program kicked back into gear. Scooting her chair backwards, she stood.

"Ma'am," her voice commanded attention. "I would suggest that when you complete your investigation and discover whoever is the guilty party, that you impose on them their punishment while making it crystal clear to the general public why this incident happened and that it would in no way stop or impede the future of the space program."

"The general public?" Miss. Blackburn's voice squawked.

"Miss Blackburn," Nicol's voice continued to command attention. "We all know what our national media's capabilities are with any bit of news they run across. At this moment, they are knocking on our door crying, "Little pig, little pig, let me come in," and waiting for the moment they can blow our house down. You have the opportunity to control what's done and what's said here. I have no desire to press charges on anyone. Nor do I have any desire to sit in a witness chair and testify against anyone.

I fully understand the magnitude of what this could have been, but I am fine. I was returned in perfect shape. It was nothing short of a miracle that you can explain in any way you choose." Nicol sat back in her chair, sucked in a deep breath, and squeezed her fingers around the warmth of her rose petal.

Silence tip-toed along the panel's table.

"Ms. Nolan, you are excused for now and we thank you for your testimony. Please, keep yourself available for further questions if that should become necessary."

"Thank you, Officer Sandlin," Nicol said. "Would it be possible, sir, for a quick trip home to re-assure my family that I am truly back on earth?"

"I think that could be arranged."

"Thank you, sir, ma'am."

George met her outside the door and walked her to his office. Inside, she collapsed into his arms.

The excitement, the stress of her time with the investigative panel, and her need to be home swallowed her in emotion.

"George," she whispered. "I need to go home."

"The arrangements are being made as we speak." Pulling his handkerchief from his back pocket, he began to gently dry her face.

When a faint trembling began, she closed her eyes and felt the pulse of a heartbeat. Opening her eyes, she smiled up at George. Peace from renewed strength chased the trembling away. She was ready for home.

CHAPTER 18

Parking at the end of the driveway, Nicol stepped from her vehicle and eyed her home. She wanted to tread carefully up the driveway and gently surprise her mother. The preacher's wife call had filled her with concern for Monica.

Drawing in a deep breath, she whispered, "God, help Mom accept the truth."

Peering through the screen door, she saw her mother sitting at the kitchen table. Although she couldn't see it, she was certain a cup of hot coffee was her only companion.

Easing the door open, she whispered across the floor. Her eyes dampened when she saw her mother's uncombed hair and trembling hands.

"Mom?"

The coffee cup shattered on the floor when Monica's chair flew backwards. Haunted eyes searched Nicol's face. Tears began to wash over the dark circles under eyes that Nicol remembered as always being bright and beautiful.

"Mom?" She gently touched her mother's arm.

"Nicol?" Monica's head shook slowly. "I didn't believe them. How could you come back?"

Nicol wrapped her arms around Monica and rocked her trembling body like a mother comforting a terrified child.

"I'm home, Mom," Nicol murmured. "I'm really home."

Monica's trembling calmed and she pulled back slightly to look into her daughter's eyes. Her smile restored life to her eyes.

Nicol took her hand and began walking toward the door. "Come on, Mom, let's sit on the porch. I certainly have missed my swing."

Nicol's arm lay across her mother's shoulders as Monica's hand rested on Nicol's thigh.

"We're going to have to work on these roses, Mom," Nicol said. "They've missed us, huh?"

Monica nodded. "Loneliness has almost killed us all." Tears slowly dampened her cheeks.

"Mom, I want to show you something."

"What would that be, Sweetie?" Monica asked.

Nicol's fingers dug into her jacket pocket and pulled out a purple velvet pouch. Pouring out its contents into the palm of her hand, she held it out to her mother.

"Is that a rose petal?" Monica asked. A strange excitement crept into her voice.

"Yes, ma'am, it certainly is."

"Where on earth did you find a purple rose? We searched everywhere and couldn't find one."

"Who searched everywhere?" Nicol asked in disbelief.

"Stephen and I searched everywhere," she said. "He was determined to find one so everywhere either of us went we would look for one."

"Oh, Mom..." Monica's fingers picked up the tiny petal.

Nicol's gasp caused her to almost drop the petal.

"What?" she exclaimed. Unlike the petal's transformation in every other human hand it had touched, the purple deepened and the gold glittered in Monica's fingers.

"Mom, do I have a story for you."

Cradling the petal from Heaven in her hand, she searched her daughter's face.

"Tell me, Nicol."

"Mama, Stephen gave me the rose this petal came from."

Monica's fingers slowly closed around the petal and her hand rested against her heart. Unable to speak, her eyes begged for the rest of the story.

"I'm assuming you know about what happened to me up there."

Monica nodded.

"Somehow my tether came loose and I drifted too far away to be rescued. I don't remember too much about that because I apparently lost consciousness within seconds."

Unable to sit still during the telling of the following events, Nicol began to pace the porch.

"The first thing I was aware of is standing on firm ground. Hands with horrible scars in them, lifted my helmet. I didn't know who had taken my helmet, but it was gone and I was dressed in a simple but fabulous gown of the softest material I've ever felt."

The swing remained motionless. Monica's hand trembled over her heart.

"And there was Nathan. Mama, he wasn't little and he wasn't exactly a man, but he was definitely Nathan. And Stephen was there."

"Where, Nicol? Where were they?"

"In Heaven, Mom, we were in Heaven."

Tears began to roll down her cheeks. Nicol scooted back into the swing, twisting to face her mother.

"Nathan held my hand and led me around showing me what I was allowed to see. The beauty of the colors and the flowers were beyond explanation. And the music, Mom, it was everywhere."

"Mom, Daddy was there, too." Silent sobs shook her body.

Monica smiled.

"I didn't know, but he was so very happy. And you know what he told me when I asked him about you?"

Still smiling, Monica shook her head.

"He said that they didn't have your mansion finished yet. He'd been checking to make sure it had everything you like."

Joyous laughter rang across the porch. "Just like your father," Monica said.

"Stephen gave me the most beautiful purple rose before I had to leave. This is one of the petals."

Holding the petal out in the palm of her hand, Monica caressed its softness.

"How?" she whispered.

"When it was time, they led me to where I first found myself. Suddenly, I was in my spacesuit again. And, Mom, this time, He stood in front of me with my helmet."

"Who?" Monica's eyebrows drew together.

"Jesus," Nicol murmured. "Jesus' scarred hands placed my helmet over my head. I looked into His eyes, Mom."

Monica's hand covered her mouth.

"I wanted to bow down and worship Him, but He held me up and told me that I still had a job to do. I thanked Him and told Him how much I love Him. He promised to be with me always."

"Oh, Nicol." Monica's hands encased her daughter's which held the petal. Feeling the heartbeat, she gasped.

"You feel it?!" Nicol exclaimed. "That's Jesus' heartbeat, Mom. When I touched his scars, I felt it. And just as the visors of my helmet closed, I remembered Stephen's rose. I almost panicked, but the last words I heard were, "You'll find what you need."

"Sure enough, this petal was in my pocket when I returned to the ship." Her finger stroked the petal.

"This is the oddest thing, Mom," Nicol said. "When everyone else, besides me, and now you, has touched this petal, it has become a cold, dead piece of stone."

"So, your dad's still watching out for me, huh?" Monica said. Her voice was just above a whisper.

Nicol nodded. "Mom, I am so sorry you had to go through such grief by yourself. And I'm sorry I caused part of it."

"Sweet girl, you didn't cause any of it. You didn't unhook your own tether."

"No, but..." Nicol fingers rubbed against the petal.

"What happens now? Do they know who was responsible?" Monica asked.

"There's this huge investigation going on; don't know how long that's going to take," Nicol said. "I just want it all to go away. I'm all right and I don't want to know who is responsible. Mom, I just want the shuttle vacation program to be a success."

Dusk slipped quietly and quickly over the mountain. Sweet, cool air whispered across the porch. Nicol slipped from the swing and walked to the front steps, sitting on the top one. One by one, bright stars, like holes in Heaven, began to appear.

"You're going back up, aren't you?" Nicol didn't turn to look. A smile lit up her face like a rosy spotlight.

"Mom, you can't possibly know what it's like up there. When God made this earth, He filled it with so much beauty. This globe hangs out in space like a rose amongst a sea of day lilies.

To me they will always be stars. Trillions of bright blinking stars sparkle against the darkness of space like diamond studded velvet. Even after what happened, there's no fear."

Monica sat beside her, draping her arm around her shoulders.

"Jesus and His Father must have had more fun that we can even imagine when they made this universe."

The women sat quietly, gazing into the star studded heavens.

"Mom?" Nicol asked.

"Yes, dear."

"Jesus sent me back for a reason. How am I going to find out what that reason is? What do you suppose He wants me to do?"

"Only you will have to figure that out, honey," Monica said.

"Whatever it is, I don't want to lose it nor do I want to waste it, Nicol said."

Dark clouds crept across the night sky, darkening the sparkles and the shine from the moon.

"You know," Monica said. "You do have an amazing testimony. Think about how God brought you out the blackness of grief, how He drew you into space, and how He allowed your visit on the other side of space. How can you use that to touch people's lives?"

The darkness was thick enough to cut, but the women remained in its shroud.

"Mom," Nicol whispered. "You're an angel. I've been keeping a journal for a while now, just so I won't forget any moment of my adventure. Whether I'm to write a book, or speak, or make a movie, God wants me to tell others."

"I think you're right, darlin'," Monica said, giving her daughter a squeeze.

"Oh, that's what daddy always called me, even up there." Nicol helped her mother stand. "Mom, I love you more that I can possibly say."

"The feeling in mutual, sweet girl."

Without the usual going-to-bed chatter, mother and daughter sought the softness of their beds. Neither would awaken until well after dawn.

CHAPTER 19

Alex Herald had been charged with the attempted murder of Nicol Nolan and an act of terrorism. The third day of the trial, Alex had been kept in his jail cell because of health issues that caused him to collapse in the courtroom the day before.

"Think we should tell her?" whispered Sandra.

The room was paneled in mahogany. Slowly rotating ceiling fans hung lower than the white globes that shed light over the room. Padded chairs lined both long tables; the judge's bench rose from the wine-colored carpet like a cathedral's dais.

Attention to detail was important in the furnishing of the hearing room, except for the acoustics. Microphones covered each long table and the judge's bench. Knowing their voices would not travel to the front, but allowing fear to wrap their voices in whispers, Sandra and Barbara leaned toward each other in their padded chairs on the back row.

Feeling as if her dragon was slithering up her back, Barbara slowly rubbed her back against the back of her chair. Shaking her head, she answered, "I don't know. She's been through so much already. Look at her."

Two rows from the front, Nicol sat with her eyes closed and her fingers massaging her temples. *Everything I didn't want to happen is happening. How do I stop this?*

"She's always trusted everyone," Sandra whispered. "If we tell her, she might just leave the space program."

"Which would be disastrous."

Like a school marm on a discipline mission, Sandra straightened in her chair and bit down on her lower lip. "We can't let this happen to her without any warning. We have to tell her."

Barbara's pinkie curled toward Sandra's. They both nodded. Barbara's dragon slept once more.

The whispering duo jumped as if shot when a tall, slim man, dressed in the uniform of a police officer, burst through the double doors.

All eyes followed the officer's quick approach to the thigh-high swinging gate guarding the proceeding arena.

"Approach, Judge?"

The fingers of her outstretched hand beckoned him forward. "This better be important." The look in his eyes answered that question.

Having delivered the manila envelope and received a, "thank you," from the judge, the officer exited as quickly as he had entered, leaving a spell of silence as all eyes now focused on the judge.

Slicing open the envelope, the judge quickly read the contents. Her eyes closed for more than a blink. Pulling in a long breath, holding it, and slowly exhaling, she stood.

"Ladies and gentlemen, we will be in recess until ten o'clock tomorrow morning. Counsel, in my chambers." Her order was terse. "Miss Nolan, follow counsel to my chamber, please."

The small audience scrambled to their feet as the judge stood. Sandra and Barbara's pinkies, still clasped, tightened.

"What?" Nicol whispered. Sliding out of her row and down the aisle to the front, she hurried through the gate held open by the bailiff. The heartbeat she felt pulsed peace through her being.

The small parade filed into the judge's chambers where the lady in the black robe was already seated behind her massive desk.

"Please, sit."

Shocked into silence, they waited.

CHAPTER 20

"Ms. Nolan, gentlemen, we have a situation, and this," she handed a legal sized envelope toward Nicol, "is said to have more evidence."

"Whoa, wait a moment," the defense counsel stood.

"Sit down and be quiet, Mr. Davis," the judge ordered. "Alex Herald is dead."

"What? No," Nicol gasped.

"Excuse me?" Mr. Davis said.

"Gentlemen, Ms. Nolan, Alex Herald was found in his cell an hour ago. It looks as if he hung himself…"

"No," moaned Nicol.

"This envelope was left with a note to whomever should find his body. It is for Nicol Nolan's eyes only and would give evidence to end this trial."

"Ms. Nolan, please." The letter remained in the judge's outstretched hand.

Walking around her desk, she pulled two tissues from the box on the desk and handed all three items to Nicol.

Nicol took the letter and slowly opened it. With a shaky voice, she read:

Dear Nicol,

As Eve in the garden of Eden, we all face times of temptation when we make decisions that will either benefit or destroy. Although I didn't realize until too late, my choice has done almost as much damage as Eve's. Because I can not find a way to live with what I have done, I want to do what I can to fix the damage by telling the truth before I leave here to face the only judge that matters.

Before we were put together as a team on the shuttle's new mission, I basically, only knew of you and your accomplishments. Jaylee and I dated for about a year, and I thought I was in love with her. I knew that she had a jealousy problem with you and a couple of the other female trainees.

Jaylee thought that if someone messed with your vehicle, you'd be scared back to Kentucky and she'd have a better chance at your job. For her sweet benefits, I arranged to have your vehicle vandalized. Then, when we were put on the first team together, Jaylee accepted my marriage proposal and promised a large amount of money if I would "accidentally" leave you up there somehow. Of course, later she told me she was only joking. Because I was insanely stupid, I thought I would give her a special wedding present and give her what she wanted. I thought I was smart enough to cause an "accident" that no one would ever be able to figure out. But, during our training and our flight, I got to know you and learned to respect and admire you. The moment I saw you sailing away from the ship, I knew I would be eternally damned. When I returned home and discovered a large unanimous deposit in my bank account, I hated Jaylee.

I know it was a miracle for you to return like you did. I also know that I'll never be forgiven for doing what I did. I know what this new space program means to you and I cannot apologize deeply enough for the damage I've done to that and consequently to you. I'll forever be thankful that you were given back to us and to the space program.

The Good Book says something about knowing the truth and it setting you free. Well, now that you know the truth, I hope in my soul that you will be set free to take the space program far into a fantastic future.

Although it seems a paltry offering, I apologize for what I have done to you, what I have done to the space program. It's too much for anyone to forgive.

I hope you will be given the opportunity to make this vacationing in the stars a reality and be honored for your achievements.

I have only one request. Please, ask the authorities to publish the truth in the news so that no one will ever have to fear space travel again.

Alex

Nicol stood; the letter fluttered to the floor. Without a word, her eyes locked on the door. She exited the room, the building, and the darkness of disappointment that had shrouded her life for far too long.

CHAPTER 21

Excitement bubbles coursing through her body, Nicol closed her eyes and asked for divine protection on the long awaited first true vacation with the stars. Two passengers would be the first civilians to experience a walk in the far away reaches of space.

Nicol thoughts floated to her visit on the other side of space. A smile lifted the corners of her lips. *Wish I could see you again, sweet Nathan.*

Following that sweet thought, a spark of dark remembrance wiggled into her mind. Furrows crossed her brow. *What? Too much has happened, but something, something…what?*

Nation media had gone wild with news of Trevor and Lori August. Not only was the couple the first ones to ride the shuttle into space, they were making the trip their honeymoon.

In the excitement of the trip and the smothering attention from the media, Trevor and Lori had given no thought to the shuttle's lack of a honeymoon suite. And now their hearts were racing. Passion was not the culprit. Panic threatened to keep Lori from being the first to step outside the shuttle.

What on earth have I sign up for? Oh, wait a second, it's not earth. Lori's sudden giggle broke the tension. At the instant of ignition, Trevor winked at his wife before the Gs grabbed his attention.

If I should ever lose this feeling of excitement, I'll retire. Nicol loved the rush, the pull of the Gs, the anticipation of being out there in God's galaxy, and the memories.

It was possibly the first time anyone had ever experienced it, but Nicol was fast asleep by the time the shuttle eased into her orbit.

Reduced to the need for a handful of controllers, mission control was now a much smaller theater. "I believe she's asleep. How is that possible?" George's voice boomed across the room.

Laughter chased his voice back to him. "Sir, that's what I call relaxed. We can't ask for much better than that," Barbara said with a smile and a wink at Sandra.

"She better get some sleep. Her first walk is in two hours," Sandra said. "Being responsible for those two love-birds is going to be a trip in itself."

Paul entered Nicol's dream, reaching for her with tears rushing down his face, trying to warn her. He was too far away, she couldn't hear. A hand with long, blood-red fingernails, grabbed her arm. When she felt fingernails scrape across the sleeve of her uniform, her arm jerked like a prize-fighter.

"Oh, I'm sorry." It was Lori's voice.

Nicol's eyes popped open. Her heart pounded like Thumper's foot. "What?" Sitting up straight, her eyes tried to focus.

"Nicol, I'm so sorry. I didn't mean to startle you."

"Lori, I apologize," Nicol said with giggle. "I was having a nightmare."

"Not about this trip, I hope." The anxiety in her voice scratched like sandpaper.

"No, Lori, no." It was Nicol's hand this time, squeezing Lori's arm.

Alex, you so didn't have to die. There's always a better way. Jaylee is in prison, where she should be. I'll do my best to help make this journey the first of hundreds.

"Lori, it's about time to get ready for our walk out there in God's world. Are you ready?" Excitement covered each word.

"Yes, ma'am," Lori said. "I admit, I'm scared, but I think it's a good scared."

"I understand. Let's go back and get started."

Trevor followed to help his wife with her EMU, giving her a sweet honeymoon kiss. She was ready, smiling like a little girl at her first dance.

The mission control monitors kept a close watch on Lori's heart rate and respiration as she made her way from inside the shuttle to the vast expanse of the universe.

Nicol couldn't help herself. Her eyes kept checking the tether. Before they made their way outside the bay, she felt the need to touch the connection just to be certain.

Looking toward Lori, her heart skipped a beat; Lori was as still as a rubber doll. "Lori, give me a sign." She tried to keep the edge of fear out of her voice. "Lori."

"I'm in awe." Lori's voice was one step beyond a whisper.

"How could anyone not believe in God in the middle of something so incredible?"

Keeping watch on her first passenger, Nicol smiled. Last time I didn't have a choice. This time, I'd give anything to soar free.

"Nicol, I will love my husband forever for giving me this gift." Lori's voice gushed with awe-filled love.

"At this point in time, Lori, you are the only bride that has ever been given this wedding gift. You are one fortunate lady." Nicol giggled.

"I am that, for sure," Lori said. "I wish he could be out here with me."

"We'll bring him out soon." Nicol said. Turning to look toward the tether connection, a warning nudged her senses. What was that? Her eyes scanned their area of the shuttle. Still jumpy, I suppose. No! George! I saw him with his arm around another woman just before we boarded. That's it! That's what's been bothering me. There's got to be an explanation.

Floating next to Lori, she began pointing out features on earth. All too soon, her signal to re-enter the shuttle sounded.

"Oh, not already," Lori whined.

"Afraid so. These memories will change your life. Let's go."

Lori's body trembled as she was assisted in removing her EMU. The moment she was free, her arms snaked around Trevor's neck. Tears soaked into the collar of his jumpsuit. "Thank you, thank you, thank you," she whispered against his neck.

"We have one hour before your walk, Trevor," Lori said. "Still want to go?"

"Are you kidding?" he said. "I wish I had gone first."

Lori pulled away from him. "Uh-huh. Jealousy has crept in." She giggled as she made her way to their special honeymoon sleeping cubicle.

Trevor winked as he followed.

CHAPTER 22

Needing to think, Nicol strapped herself into her seat and closed her eyes. Knowing that this was out of character for Nicol when she was on a flight, the crew kept watch, just in case.

The furrows creased her forehead once more as she allowed the memory to re-enter her thoughts. Who was she? Even from the back she looked familiar. I'm certain he was only trying to calm her. Her head slowly moved back and forth. He kissed her head. No! Her fist slammed the arm rest as her lips pursed and her eyes opened.

"Nicol, you okay?" Jonathan Armstrong, the captain, asked.

"Yes, sir," she said. "Sometimes, useless thoughts thunder though like a space locomotive, you know." Her giggle wasn't convincing.

"Yes, ma'am, I know." Everyone has known but her. I don't care how many strips he carries, someone needs to..."

"Time to suit up, Nicol?" Trevor asked.

"What's the matter, Trev?" she asked, smiling. "You anxious?"

"Lori hasn't stopped talking yet," he said. "Yes, I'm more anxious than ever."

"Let's get started then." Nicol made her way to begin donning her EMU.

"Oh, Trevor, I'm so excited for you," Lori gushed as she helped him with his EMU. Touching his face for the last time, she whispered, "Come back to me, you hear?"

"I promise." His wink touched her heart as much as a kiss.

Nicol and Trevor moved through the first set of doors to finish each step of the process before floating out into space.

Nicol drew in a deep breath. This is where I love to be. Checking their tethers, she floated out.

Just as they moved past the edge of the shuttle, Trevor touched her puffy sleeve. "Nicol, is that normal?" He gestured to the area in front of the bay doors. A dark square seemed to yawn at them like a missing tooth.

Oh my! That's the darkness that tried to grab my attention earlier. What's going on with me?

"Jonathan, we have a problem out here."

"You two look okay, what's up?" Refusing to allow panic to invade his voice, the captain's eyes darted around the area where Trevor and Nicol were.

Nicol swallowed a lump the size of a small asteroid. "Sir, it appears that two tiles are missing."

February 1, 2003, flashed in his mind like neon arrows. "Bring your passenger in and I'll send Paul out to take a look."

"Yes, sir," Nicol said. Turning to advise Trevor, her heart thudded against her rib cage. No Trevor.

"Nicol! I'm over here," Like a school boy playing hide-and-go-seek, Trevor began waving from near the portal that would take them back inside.

Nicol maneuvered her way to Trevor. Unable to see his face, she was thankful that he also could not see hers. "We have to go in, Trevor."

"I thought as much," he said. "It's kind of drab out here anyway."

"Drab?" Nicol was shocked. "You honestly think this is drab?"

"Pretty much," Trevor said just as the door opened.

"Paul, if you'll get Mr. Trevor taken care of, I'll re-check the damage."

Paul helped Trevor through the door so that no damage would be done to his EMU. Many long, lonely minutes later, Nicol caught a peripheral glimpse of Paul's white EMU as he maneuvered to her side.

"Paul, please tell me we have what it takes to replace these tiles. I love it out here, but I also want to make it home."

"We trained for this type of repair, Nicol," Paul answered. "It will take both of us to git-er-done." Hearing fear edge her words, he tried to lighten the situation.

"You trained for repairs; I trained to space walk our passengers," Nicol said.

"I remember something about you aceing everything," Paul said. "Follow my lead and I'll make an expert repair man out of you."

"Oh, thanks," she said. "Just what I always wanted to do."

"Follow me and we'll get the super glue." He maneuvered to the inside of the bay.

"Super glue?" Nicol exclaimed. "You are joking, right?"

"Sort of," Paul said. Opening a numbered door in the bay area, he pulled two quilt-type bags out, handing Nicol one.

"Here we go."

Chewing on her lower lip, Nicol followed.

Both astronauts were as quiet as space until they reached the black squares on the side of the shuttle. Paul stopped and faced Nicol.

"Listen, Nicol," he said. "Other than our training, neither of us have had to do this, and whether we do this correctly or not depends on if we get home safely. I know you pray, so this might be a good time to say a really good prayer."

"Father, God, we need your help here. Satan is trying to destroy us and our mission. It's not that I'd mind seeing you, but we're responsible for several people up here. Please, guide us as we make these repairs. Where we might fail, I'm asking you to fix those spots. In fact, I'll go ahead and ask that you keep all of the tiles on our ship just where they need to be and cover them with your protection so that when we make re-entry, all of us and the shuttle will be safe. Thank you, God, for hearing and for your help. Jesus, I'm asking this in your name with praise and gratitude. Amen."

"All right, it's time to go to work," Paul said as he slid what he called his glue-gun from the bag. "You have the extra tiles. I'm going to apply this, we'll wait the required minutes, then you and I will place each tile slowly. Got it?"

"Yes, sir," she said. Quietly watching, she was amazed that the "glue" actually stuck on the shuttle and didn't snake off into space like a long worm. Quicker than she expected, the glue was waiting for the tiles.

"Tell us when, captain," Paul said while he managed to get the glue gun back into the bag. Nicol watched as he fastened the bag onto his belt. Whether he considered himself an expert or not, she was impressed with how adept he was at the task before him.

"One minute," the captain said.

"Ready?" Paul asked, turning to Nicol.

"Yes, sir," she said.

"To make certain that each tile is applied correctly, we have to do this as if we were one. Just follow my lead."

As carefully as handling a pane of glass, Paul removed the first tile and closed the bag so the others would not drift out and away. "Okay, you hold that side, I'll hold this. We lay it in one smooth motion. Ready?"

"Let's do it," she said.

The tile could not have been placed more perfectly if they had been doing this all of their lives.

"Wow," she whispered. "Thank you, Jesus."

"How about thank you, Paul?"

"That, too." Her giggle relaxed both of them.

"One more." Paul reached into the bag.

"Just like the other one, God," Nicol whispered.

As if angels guided their movements, the tile settled into its spot.

"Thank you, Jesus," Paul said.

Nicol smiled.

"Well..." he said. "That definitely was easy."

"Miracles usually are, sir." Nicol said.

"If you say so." He said it to be flippant, but she recognized the unspoken awe.

Lifting her eyes to the darkness of space, she winked.

"Let's get inside?" Paul's voice pulled her attention back to the present.

"I am so ready," she said.

"Could I speak to you privately, Nicol?" Lori smiled, but there was no mistaking the fear jumping in her eyes.

Nicol giggled. "As privately as possible, Mrs. August." Her signature giggle most generally put people at ease.

Moving to a spot near the sleeping cocoons, the girls spoke as privately as possible in the confines of the space shuttle.

"Nicol, I'm having a major meltdown the closer we get to re-entry."

"Fear is a totally normal emotion for any space traveler—male or female, professional or tourist."

"Oh, you don't understand," Lori whispered.

Nicol saw and felt the intensity of Lori's trembling body.

"This could be labeled panic, pure, heart-stopping panic."

With the tenderness of a mother's touch, Nicol placed her hands on Lori's shoulders. "I have the remedy for that." Her eyes smiled with the compassion of Jesus.

"I really don't want to take any medication, but I'm terrified that I'm going to stroke out here."

Nicol laughed. "You are so funny. No, Lori, what I have is not medication. I'd like to pray for you." Her eyebrows rose, waiting for Lori's agreement.

"Yes, oh, yes." Relief leapt from her eyes.

"Good, because this is the remedy. Medication covers up problems, this speaks healing."

CHAPTER 23

Like a pool of piranha, the media swirled around the room, their cameras clicking like bloody teeth.

As if she were afflicted with nystagmus, Nicol's eyes darted through the crowd. *Where is he? Were the girls right?*

"Nicol, how did your initial space walk disaster affect this walk? How frightened were you? Did your fear affect your first two paying customers?"

"It never ceases to amaze me how reporters can garble so many questions into one. First answer – I would love to re-experience my first space walk adventure. Second answer – no, I was not frightened, therefore answer number three would be a no. My first two civilian space walkers experienced excitement, just like I did."

Like a deflating balloon, the pretty, young reporter shriveled into her chair with a I'll-get-you-later glare at Nicol.

"Mr. and Mrs. August, given the opportunity on your first wedding anniversary, would you return to space for another walk with the stars?" One of the older reporters would attempt to pull the answers he could use to the advantage of his writing.

"No, sir," Trevor said. "I wouldn't pay that much to be bored again."

Lori's head swiveled to face him. "Bored? Our honeymoon?" Her voice was just above a whisper.

Laughter skipped over the room.

"Excuse me, Trevor, surely you're not saying your honeymoon was boring?"

"No, no, of course not," Trevor said as his arm pulled his bride close. "The honeymoon was beyond words. The space walk was a bit boring. I guess I've watched too many space odysseys on TV."

"And you, Lori?" The reporter was relentless.

"My mind is still in the process of compartmentalizing my experience, which I can assure you was in no way boring. Once I was out in space, the beauty was breath-taking, or maybe I should say oxygen-taking."

A spattering of laughter skipped over the room.

"I experienced an overwhelming desire to take off my puffy suit and sail among the stars for a while."

"You mean, like your space hostess did on her first step out of the shuttle?" The pretty, young reporter interjected.

Lori's eyes bore into the reporter's, making her cheeks flame.

"No, ma'am, not like that at all. Nicol kept her suit on and she did not voluntarily sail through space."

"Thank you. That will be all the questions at this time. Good evening," the emcee announced.

As Nicol and the Augusts were herded into the hallway, Nicol's intent was to scoot down the hall to find George. It was time to put her fears to rest.

Lori snagged her arm and refused to let go. Nicol's jaws tightened. "You okay?" she asked, feeling like a trapped animal.

Lori nodded. "I just need to thank you."

"That's not necessary, Lori. Just doing my job."

"No, it is necessary. You went far and beyond your job requirements. Through you, I am learning to see what I need to see, to hear what I need to hear, and to hope when I had no reason to before."

Nicol wrapped Lori in her arms as if she were a long-lost child.

"Oh, Lori, it wasn't me. With your new relationship with God, you're going to be given many, many more blessings from the Giver of all blessings." Pulling back, she held Lori's shoulders. "You have my contact information if you ever just need to talk."

Unable to speak, Lori nodded.

Placing a kiss on her forehead, Nicol winked and walked down the hallway.

"Okay, God, if you can do that, you can fix this."

George's voice and a female voice seeped through the closed door. Nicol's knock turned off the volume.

"Nicol!" George exclaimed upon opening the door. Grasping her upper arms, his chin bumped her forehead as he tried to kiss it. "Come in. Come in."

He had not missed the stiffness of her limbs and movements. Her feet moved slowly across the gray carpet.

"Nicol, this is Kristine Cleek, Head Agent for Homeland Security here at Johnson, uh, excuse me, Galaxy Training Center.

Extending her small, well manicured hand in Nicol's direction, Kristine's slim, well-proportioned body leaned slightly forward. "Honored to meet you. I've heard lots about you, Nicol. May I call you Nicol?"

Her reluctance dissipated like a sun-heated fog when their hands met. "It's a pleasure. And, yes, Nicol is fine."

The warmth of Kristine's hand matched the warmth in her brown eyes. Blond hair curved around the collar of her navy-colored jacket.

"Please, ladies." George gestured toward the chairs facing his desk. "I haven't seen you around here before, is there a problem now?"

"Just routine checks. Even though Galaxy operates the program, the government has to keep an eye on every aspect. Can't allow surprises." Kristine's eyes darted toward George.

The peace of the now familiar heart beat when she looked at George chased away the dread, jealousy, and the fear. Nicol smiled.

George took a deep, cleansing breath.

"It looked as if your first vacation with the stars was a complete success," Kristine said.

"It was amazing," Nicol said. "The new husband was a bit of a fuddy-dud, but the bride's experience will stay with her for a lifetime."

"Great," Kristine exclaimed. "With all the civilians that will be entering the program, my job is going to become more complicated. Security issues always intensify when the public becomes involved in projects such as this."

"I'm sure," Nicol said, relaxing against the back of her chair. "I would imagine that the money Galaxy has invested in this entire project will be returned much faster than even they expected."

"That's exactly one of the issues we," she nodded in George's direction, "have been discussing. If that should happen, and by the way, this information stays in this room, it's a real possibility that the United States Space Program will again be sole owners and operators of the Program."

"Now, that's exciting news." Nicol's eyes sparkled. "It has always been my belief that the Space Program should be under the complete control of the United States. The biggest issue in that department would be the media's role in the entire project."

Kristine winked at George. "We are presently working on a plan, in the utmost secrecy I might add, to use their tactics to our benefit."

"Really? If I can help, just call." Nicol's laughter was sweet. "Speaking of calling, George, I will be leaving this evening for Kentucky. I have papers to sign and some good-byes to take care of before moving my mother closer. And all this before my next mission."

"Wow, Nicol, that in itself sounds like a mission." Kristine stood to shake her hand again.

"I guess you could say that," Nicol said. "It has been a real pleasure. Thank you for everything you're doing to keep us safe. Hope to see you again."

"Without a doubt."

"I'll call when I return," Nicol said to George.

"I'll be waiting." He walked her to the door with his arm around her waist, but did not kiss her.

CHAPTER 24

Just before leaving for Kentucky, Nicol had found a perfect beachside cottage for herself and her mother in the Cocoa Beach area of Florida. The fully furnished quaint little cottage had belonged to an elderly couple who had recently passed away. The family had no desire for the cottage and after meeting Nicol, gave her one of those offers that couldn't be passed up.

Legal papers in Kentucky were signed, only their personal items they wanted to keep were packed, and the last trip to the hillside cemetery was made. The trip to Florida was fast and sweet. Monica was as excited as a teenager heading into a new adventure.

Their first morning in their new home, mother and daughter sat at the glass-topped table looking out the screen door toward the ocean.

"Can you believe this, Mom?" Nicol asked. "In one week's time, God sold our Kentucky home, gave us this amazing cottage on the beach with a view like that, and we're already moved in."

"Only God can do miracles like that," Monica said, sipping her hot tea. "Just to think that every morning we're going to see this."

"Wow," Nicol said.

"Wow is right," Monica said. "I'm going to miss my mountains, but God has provided even more beauty for me."

"And I still have a week left of my vacation," Nicol said. "I can't wait to take a walk on the beach."

"You know what I'm going to do?" Monica asked. Her hands lay flat on the table.

"What would that be, young lady," Nicol said. "Go on a beach walk with me?"

"No, ma'am," she said. "I'm going back to bed."

"What? Are you kidding me?" Nicol said. "You never go back to bed."

"Well, it's about time I started." Monica placed her empty cereal bowl and tea cup in the sink. "Lying on that bed in front of my window facing the ocean is going to be wonderful."

"Sure you're feeling all right," Nicol asked. Her smile was on her lips only.

"Better than ever. Thank you darlin' for this." Monica kissed the top of her daughter's head before going to her bedroom.

"Definitely my pleasure." Watching her mother disappear into her bedroom, Nicol's clasped hands tightened in her lap. She has never called me darlin'.

"Enjoy your walk," Monica called through the screen as Nicol headed out on to the beach.

Bending to pick up one more shell to add to her collection, Nicol's rose petal swished across her chin. George had taken the petal to the best jeweler in the area and had it mounted on a sterling silver chain. Completely lost in the beauty of her walk through the warm sand with her fingers wrapped around the purple petal, she'd lost all track of time.

"Oh dear," she whispered, looking at her watch. Turning around, she was only able to see her cottage through the mist. "I must have walked a mile. Mom." Choosing to move up on the beach where the sand was firm, she jogged back to her starting point.

"Mom, I'm home," she called.

"Hi, honey, that you?" Hearing the joy in her mother's voice made her smile. Thank you, Jesus.

"I have an apple pie in the oven," Monica sang out. "It will be hot and ready in a bit."

"Oh, yummy," Nicol said. Walking into the kitchen she wrapped her arms around her mother. "I'm going to take a quick shower first. Don't eat it all while I'm gone."

"Well, you just never know," Monica said.

Just as she reached for the water knob, her cell phone jingled. "Shoot! It will wait." Her body was soon covered with warm, silky water. The phone rang again. "Must be important." Snatching a towel from the rack, she wrapped it quickly. "Hello."

"I need to see you." Urgency pushed through the phone.

"George?"

"I need to see you," he repeated.

"I'm home." Her eyebrows drew together.

"Good, be there in a few." No good-bye or see you later, just dead space.

"Alrighty then." She dressed, dabbed on makeup, and fixed her hair before meeting her mother in the kitchen.

"That was quick," Monica said.

"George, called. He's on his way over."

"Great, the pie is done and it will be cooled and ready for him. He must have missed you." Her smile was mischievous.

"Actually, I don't know if this is a social visit, or if something is going on. He sounded a little strange," Nicol said.

"H-m-m-m. A little mystery is sweet."

Nicol's laughter was contagious. While they were sharing their happiness, the doorbell rang.

CHAPTER 25

"Monica, that was a gift from Heaven," George said. Like a kitten after eating, he licked his lips.

Monica's eyes sparkled as she touched his cheek.

George's eyes sought Nicol's and found them smiling in dampness. "Is it too late for a beach walk?" he asked

"Oh, I'd love it," Nicol exclaimed. "Mom, want to join us?" Kissing her mother's cheek, she noticed a little extra warmth.

"Actually, no, but I will go sit in my chair and keep an eye on you young folks."

George sat on the couch to remove his loafers and roll up his slacks. "Young folks?" he said. "Nicol failed to tell me about your bad eyesight, Monica." He laughed.

Monica patted his shoulder. "I remember my grandmother saying that to me and my fella not that long ago. Never thought I'd actually say it myself." Her laughter was as sweet as spring rain.

George carried the chair with one hand and held Monica's hand with the other. As she locked the door, Nicol leaned her forehead against its coolness and shook her head.

Holding the chair while Monica settled, George asked, "All set?"

"Yes, sir, that I am," Monica said.

Silent as a falling snowflake, Nicol squatted next to her mother, watching her eyes. Monica was seeing something Nicol could not. Her voice was soft and breathy.

"Out there," Monica's arm fanned across her outstretched legs, "there's nothing between. Almost as if I can reach out and touch Him."

George placed his hand under Nicol's elbow. In slow motion she stood. She pulled in a shaky breath.

"Sure you'll be ok, Mom?"

"Yes, ma'am." Monica smiled up at her daughter. "You kids go have your walk. I'll be fine."

"Ok," Nicol forced happiness into her voice. "Need anything, buzz my phone."

"Oh! Oh, Nicol." Monica waved her hands like a prima dona. "Do you have your petal?"

"Why, yes," Nicol answered. Her brows pulled together as she fished her necklace from inside her blouse. Why would she ask that now?

"Would you mind if I held on to it for you. I'd hate for it to get lost out there in the sand." Monica said.

"Certainly, Mom." She slipped the chain from her neck and placed it on her mother's. "Guard it with your life." Nicol said softly.

Monica's fingers wrapped around the purple treasure. "You know it, darlin'." She took a deep breath and closed her eyes. "Now, scoot while the sun still shines."

George entwined his fingers with Nicol's. Silence followed their steps to the water's edge. George waited.

A tear sparkled on her cheek. "Oh, to see what she saw," she whispered.

Slipping his arm around her waist, he pulled her against his side. "After that experience, it's going to be difficult telling you what I came here for."

"Let's walk." Making occasional checks over her shoulder so they wouldn't go too far, she encouraged him to open up.

"You know I'm not a weak-kneed blond girl, right?" she asked.

His laughter allowed her to relax. "What I'm going to tell you has the highest clearance. That's why I needed to talk to you where listening ears could not hear."

"Okay, kiss me." Nicol said, swinging around to face him and wrapping her arms around his neck.

"What?" He was shocked into paralysis.

"Make it look real." She giggled as she rose up on her toes and waited for his response.

"Okay." A quick smile broke his paralysis. Pulling her tightly to him, he made it look real.

"Geez." She squeaked. "What an actor."

Pulling her even tighter, he made reality sizzle. Breaking for air, he whispered, "I'm going for an Oscar here."

Her laughter rippled like the waves.

She took his hand as they began walking. "Maybe an Emmy," she said before running ahead.

"Oh, yeah!" he shouted, chasing her as if they were teenagers.

She stopped so suddenly, he almost crashed into her.

"I'm not even a singer," he murmured against her ear.

"Yes, but you make my heart sing, Mr. Oscar." Breaking the moment, she wiggled from the hug.

"Look at that," she said. "Is that strange or what?"

"What?" He missed whatever had caught her attention.

"Look at that circle of white sand." She pointed to what looked to be a perfect three-foot circle of snow white sand. "What would cause sand to be so white right in the middle of the beach?"

Realizing that he wasn't responding, she turned. George was staring at the white circle as if it were a circle of white death. "George?"

"Can we sit?" he asked.

"Are you all right?" she asked.

"Let's walk." He took her hand and kissed it.

Acting like true lovers, they kicked through the sand toward a park bench on the top side of the beach. Sliding her arm behind his back and leaning her head against his shoulder, she said, "We should be safe here." She felt his jaw tighten. "George, please just tell me."

Not just for role playing sake he kissed the top of her head, allowing the kiss to linger. "As many years as I've worked here, I've never broken security confidentialities. Security is of the utmost importance in this program. But, you need to know. You have to know."

Nicol's eyes scanned the horizon as if expecting enemy bombers to dot the skyline. Keeping silent, she allowed him to confide national security issues with her.

"Kristene is here for a specific reason. There have been very real, very dark threats against not only our program, but against our country. We're not certain on their timeline, except that it will be soon. Our president wants to delay advising the public to avoid a panic epidemic.

"It's that serious?" Her fingers drew up into a fist.

"More so than 9-11," he said. "Since the space shuttle has again become active, we've received intel that the enemy is planning to destroy the Cape and somehow use the shuttle." He felt her body begin to tremble.

As if in slow motion, Nicol stood. After looking toward her mother, she sat in the sand and began digging like a child building a sand fort.

"I'm not going to waste time asking who. But, I do need to know if the shuttle is in danger. We have lift-off in two weeks."

George joined her in the sand. "I can't confirm or deny that."

Nicol lifted her arms to drop them over his shoulders. With eyes hidden behind her sunglasses, she scanned as much of the area behind him as possible. How would she know if someone were watching them? How would she know if sophisticated listening devices were pointed in their direction? The kiss she placed on his lips was filled with tenderness.

"Let's walk by the water." She didn't wait for him to stand first. Jumping up like a school girl, she ran toward the surf.

Weighted down with fear, George moved through the sand like a loggerhead turtle. Stepping into the water, he stood looking at the horizon with his hands on Nicol's shoulders.

Leaning back against him, she said, "We'll walk slowly back to mom. Can you fill me in by then?"

With fingers clasping fingers, they walked slowly through the waves and sand. Evening was creeping closer as the horizon changed from gray blue to red. Nearing Monica, Nicol stopped in front of George, wrapping her arms around his waist. "So, that's why the circle of white sand affected you so?"

The walk back seemed like eternity as George gave her information that filled her with more fear than her spirit could hold.

He nodded. The mixture of fear, pain, and dread creased his face.

Just before kissing him, she whispered in his ear, "That face will fool no one, no matter how powerful the camera lens are." As her lips caressed his, she felt him relax and his arms pulled her tighter.

"You'd make an excellent spy, young lady," he said against her ear. "Maybe you missed your true calling." For minutes he held her tightly. How do I calm her fears now?

Giggling, she grabbed his hand and pulled him toward her mother. "That one was as real as it gets, mister."

"Hi, Mom. Ready to go in?" Nicol chirped like a wounded sparrow.

It's hard letting go," Monica said. Her eyes were glued to the red horizon

Nicol's heart skipped a beat as she slowly sat on the edge of Monica's chair. "Excuse me?"

"Aw, Niki, you know." Monica's hands caressed her daughter's cheeks. "These moments in this world when it feels as if I can almost see Jesus. It's these feelings that are hard letting go of."

"I certainly could go for another piece of that apple pie about now," George said.

"That's just what I was thinking, young man," Monica said. "Let's see if it might still be a little warm." She swung her legs over the edge of the chair and grunted as she pushed herself up.

Nicol smiled, but George saw the glitter of a tear as he bent to fold up the chair. With a last look across the white-tipped waves, he saw what he knew was the glint of a very large camera lens from a sailboat far out in the cobalt colored water.

Walking toward the cottage, he swatted Nicol's behind. Shocked speechless, she spun around to swing her mother's beach towel in his direction. Then, she saw his eyes. Grabbing him around the waist, she pulled their bodies together. His heart ached to feel her still trembling.

Long into the moon-lit night, Nicol sat on the screened in patio listening to the waves thunder against the beach. Although the night was warm, she was wrapped in a crocheted throw. Her body refused to stop trembling. Trying to absorb everything George had shared with her was too much. An hour before the sun pushed back the darkness, she dozed.

On her way to the beach for her morning devotions, Monica failed to see her daughter. Halfway to her favorite spot, she stumbled, falling to her knees.

"Just a little further, Jesus. Just a little further." No matter how she tried, she was unable to stand. Exhausted, she lay on the damp sand and sighed. "Oh, okay, Jesus. I'll get there if you'll wait a few minutes."

Two hours passed before a dog's barking woke Nicol. What is up with that dog? Forcing herself to her feet, still wrapped in the afghan, she walked to the screen door.

A large, black Labrador Retriever lay next to a familiar form out on the sand. "Mom?" The screen door slammed open.

Thinking the dog had attacked her mother, she approached cautiously. Whining, the dog laid his head on Monica's back.

"Mom?" Nicol whispered, falling to her knees. Monica's head rested on her Bible. A smile had pulled the corners of her mouth up slightly. Nicol laid her fingers on her cool neck. "Aw, Mom, no."

Placing a kiss on her cheek, Nicol gently covered her with the afghan. The dog didn't want to move his head, but finally lifted it just enough. "You knew she was special, didn't you, boy? Thanks for watching over her." Tears ran down her cheeks.

Nicol called 911 on her cell phone and waited. The second call was to George.

While she waited, Nicol caressed her mother's hair. Through the prism of tears, she noticed Monica's hand curled into a fist. Monica's body had already cooled, but as Nicol touched her hand, she was shocked with hope to feel warmth.

"Look at this!" Nicol exclaimed. The purple rose leaf necklace fell to the sand. "That's the deepest purple it's ever been." Holding the necklace to her heart, her eyes lifted. "Thank You."

Pulling the afghan over Monica's arm and now cooled hand, she sobbed. A large black paw covered Nicol's hand. Her head lifted from her mother's body as she looked into the dog's damp eyes and smiled.

Two paramedics pushed a gurney through the sand. Before Nicol stood, she wrapped her arms around his black chest and kissed the top of his head.

Sensing completion of his job, the dog licked her cheek and slowly disappeared across the sand.

After kissing her mother's forehead before the paramedics lifted her body into the ambulance, Nicol walked out onto the beach. Shading her eyes she searched both ways for the dog.

"Oh well," she whispered. "God can do anything, even make an angel look like a big black dog."

The shuttle's launch was postponed for two weeks while Nicol took her mother back to the small family cemetery on the hill behind the Kentucky church. Church members had taken care of the family plot while she was gone.

Being in the peace of this little spot on their Kentucky mountain, she was reminded of the other side of space. The fear that threatened to destroy her, began to dissipate. After kissing each cold stone, Nicol smiled and turned to walk back into a life of unknown. Her trust in Jesus took on a new depth of hope.

Unbeknownst to Nicol, as the final week progressed toward lift-off, her cottage was emptied and the contents stored in a secure location that only George and one other person knew about.

George's footsteps echoed as he walked through the empty cottage. Standing on the patio looking across the blue waters to the glowing red ball as it sank behind the horizon, tears tumbled down his whiskered face like tiny pinballs.

"Looks as if I might possibly be seeing you soon, Lord," he prayed. "I wish I could stop this from happening, but unless you do one of your miracles, this will only be a memory. Please..." a sob caught in his chest. "Please protect her."

Feeling as if the eight arms of an octopus were wrapped around his chest, George gasped for air. "The pain is too great. Not just mine and hers but for all the others who will be affected."

Finally able to draw in a deep cleansing breath, he turned to leave the cottage. "I ask for wisdom. And, I ask for courage to face this. Jesus, it's You and Your name I am heavily relying on."

The door clicked behind him.

CHAPTER 26

It was to be a night-time launch. Strapped in her seat, Nicol could see the star-studded backdrop that would soon be their orbital destination. This launch was seriously different in the orbiter's cabin. The loss of Nicol's usual bubbly personality concerned Commander Armstrong.

Nicol closed her eyes and began her usual silent prayers as the minutes clicked by faster than seconds. Finished praying, she kept her eyes closed, remembering their last night in the cabin.

George's arms had held her long and tenderly as if she were a porcelain doll. Quietly talking next to her ear, he had said, "Remember our walks on the beach."

She nodded.

"Everything we talked about is in place. You'll understand when it's time. I promise. Duane Embree will be there for you if things go south."

Her legs felt as if they were going to fail her. Her eyes squeezed shut. He felt her heart thudding against his chest.

"If our task fails, everything along this coast will be destroyed. You will be kept safe. Remember each of the hiding places I told you about. You'll find everything you'll need."

Tears dampened his shoulder. She was unable to stop the sob that escaped her pain-constricted throat as his arms began to relax. No! Don't let go!

Slowly, he stepped back. "I've put you in the only Hands that matter."

"But, what about you?" she sobbed.

"No matter what happens here or where you are, we're both going to be in His hands, you know that."

Smiling through her tears, she had nodded. "You're right," she said. "I have to keep reminding myself of that."

"Just like the old hymn says, God be with you 'til we meet again, my love." George's voice shook.

As she had pulled in her lips, Nicol closed her eyes and held her breath. At the moment she thought she had control, she opened her eyes and the room was empty.

The porcelain doll had crumbled.

And Then...

Before the other side of space became reality, God's miracles remained strong and sure.

"I remember how impressed I was with every moment of my training on and around Alamogardo. God certainly created beautiful parts of every state in America. Even knowing how certain areas would be used for advanced war weaponry building, testing, and launches. Here the amazing white sands remain as clean and sparkling as Heaven," Nicol reminisced.

"Remember the white sand circle on the beach where you began your verbal education about the land of the white sand?"

"Do I ever!" she responded. "Who would have ever thought we would now be retired close to such a violent, beautiful place?"

"Do you ever wish for any other place?"

"No, George. It going to be far too many years for Cocoa Beach to be safe again," Nicol said. "This piece of heaven between the mountains and the white sands is perfect."

"Do you miss the job of being the first mistress of Space Walkers?" he squeezed her hand.

"Absolutely not. I enjoyed it, but that last mission ended it for me. Far too much heavy responsibility and over the top fear trying to stay safely hidden all these years was enough."

"And now?" George asked.

"Now?" she smiled. "Freedom from fear, absolute love from and with the man who protected me from day one, and makes me feel at peace always. Although these mountains aren't the same as my beloved Kentucky mountains, they are wonderful, along with clear water, white beaches, our own gardens of fresh veggies and beautiful flowers. Thank you, George, for gifting me with perfection."

"I was never able to match Stephen's gift to you from the other side of space, but this ain't shabby."

"Ain't? Maybe we've been living in the outback too long. Ain't! Really?" her laughter bounced across their chairs.

In comfy lawn chairs, holding hands, their eyes smiled their love. Nicol caressed her purple and golden edged rose necklace.

"It's a shame that the rest of the world and America has become destroyed by hate and unholy pride in the remaining leaders. Occasionally, I catch up on the news from the stations we can almost trust. After we completed the last mission we had to thwart the destruction aimed at the coast, I hoped those situations would improve. Now, I wait expectantly for Jesus to step out on the clouds any moment." George's demeanor slid into sadness.

"I agree, Honey," Nicol said. God's timing has more than proven to be different than ours. We've waited much longer than I expected. I love our sheltered piece of what's left, but I yearn more and more for the other side of space."

"While you sleep through the night, I come out here and watch the sky. Amazingly, even in the dark, it's like watching through a kaleidoscope the dance of the clouds." George kissed the back of her hand.

"I don't suppose there will be nothing from here on earth that we will miss when we get there, but if there should be, it would be the clouds. I spend hours of my days just sitting here watching them," Nicol said.

"I am so thankful for you, my darling, and for the life we have shared together. The good has far outweighed the dark and ugly." George sat on the edge of his chair so he could caress her arms and face.

"I agree one hundred percent." Nicol scooted her chair closer so they could reach each other with their love.

"Our little, well sort of little, space here has been peaceful. Especially compared to the rest of the world. Two nights ago, while out here, I felt and heard multiple rocket blasts. I was tempted to grab my phone to find out what's up. Thankfully I remembered that part of our life is over." George gently pulled her on to his lap.

"You bet," she said. "This is the best. God has given us so much, especially each other."

At peace, in love, George and Nicol fell asleep in each other's arms, as the sun slithered over the other side of the mountains.

Hours later, dawn dusted gold over the clouds of the east. Still holding each other, their eyes startled open as Heavenly trumpets blasted.

Along with untold numbers of believers

George and Nicol danced on the other side of space.

On The Other Side Of Space/Chastain/8500

And, then...

"I remember how impressed I was with every moment of my training at Alamogardo and all around the base and area. It was almost beyond belief all the weapons and such that were made, tested, and launched from the base. With all those launches and everything else, the sand remained, well remains white as snow," Nicole reminised.

"Do you remember the white sand circle on the beach where you began your verbal education about the land of the white sand?"

"Do I ever," she responded. "Who would ever have thought we would now be retired close to such a violent, beautiful place?"

"Do you ever wish for any other place?"

"No, George. It going to be far too many years for Cocoa Beach to be safe again," Nicol said. This piece of heaven between the mountains and the white sands is perfect."

"Do you miss the job you were first mistress of?" he squeezed her hand.

"Absolutely not. I enjoyed it, but the last mission ended it for me. Far too much heavy responsibility and over the top fear trying to stay hidden all these years was enough."

"And, now?" George asked.

"Now?" she smiled. "Freedom from fear, absolute love from and with the man who protected me from day one, and makes me feel as if I will never fear again will keep me forever. Mountains, clear water,

---

white beaches, our own gardens of fresh veggies and beautiful flowers. Thank you, George for giving me this gift."

"I wasn't able to match Stephen's gift to you from the other side to space, but this isn't shabby."

In comfy lawn chairs, holding hands, they smiled. Nicol caressed her purple and golden rose necklace.

"It's an absolute shame that the rest of the world and America has become destroyed by hate and unholy pride in the remaining leaders. Occasionally, I catch up on the news from stations we can almost trust. After we did what we had to do to thwart the destruction aimed at the coast, I hoped those situations would emprove. I have expected Jesus to step out on the clouds any moment."

"Me, too. God's timing has more than proven to be different than ours. We've waited much longer that I expected. I love our sheltered piece of what's left, but I yearn more and more for the other side of space," she added.

"While you sleep through the night, I come out here and watch the sky. Amazingly, even in the dark, it's like watcheing the clouds dance and tumble in a kaliedoscope."

"I suppose there is nothing from here on earth we will miss in Heaven, but if I miss anything, it will be the clouds. I spend hours of my days just watching the dance of the clouds." George said. "I am so thankful for you, my darling, and for the life we've had and have together. The good has far out weighed the dark and ugly."

"I agree one hundred per cent." She kissed his hand.

"Our little, well sort of little, space here has been peaceful. Especially compared to the rest of the world. Two nights ago, while out here, I felt and heart multiple rocket blasts. I was tempted to grab my phone to find out what's up. But, remembered. That part of our life is over."

"You bet."

At peace, in love, George and Nicol fell asleep as the sun slithered over the other side of the mountain.

Hours later, dawn dusted gold over the clouds of the east.

Still holding hands, their eyes startled open as Heavenly trumpets blasted.

George and Nicol danced on the other side of space.

Printed in the United States
by Baker & Taylor Publisher Services